BLOOD VICE

BLOOD VICE

BLOOD VICE BOOK ONE

ANGELA ROQUET

VIOLENT SIREN PRESS

BLOOD VICE

Copyright © 2017 by Angela Roquet

www.angelaroquet.com

Cover Art by Rebecca Frank

Edited by Chelle Olson of Literally Addicted to Detail

ISBN: 978-1-951603-28-1

For Paul and Xavier,

who make my world go round.

Chapter One

As I lay dying on the floor of an abandoned warehouse basement in the bowels of St. Louis, I couldn't help but question every choice I'd ever made. Which one of them had led to this moment? Was it just one? Maybe my entire life had been one poor decision after another. That seemed the most likely answer as I stared into the vacant eyes of my partner sprawled out on the concrete not ten feet away.

Will Banks had definitely drawn the short straw when it came to being paired with me. At the time, it had seemed like divine intervention. His partner was transferring to a PD down in Florida, and I was finally getting the promotion I'd had my sights set on since day one. Will had been my mother's partner ten years ago. Being paired with him felt like an omen from the universe. Like a sign from my mom even, that everything was unfolding as it should.

What a joke.

I thought of Will's wife and daughter. He'd bragged about Serena to me just that morning, about the big scholarship she'd been awarded to go into the engineering program at MU. I could remember babysitting Serena the summer Will and Alicia had moved to St. Louis. I'd been sixteen, and she had just turned five. She was all bubblegum cheeks and beaded cornrows, full of exciting facts from her family's recent trip to the Gateway Arch. That was twelve years ago. Had so much time really passed?

I was finally able to think of something worse than dying in a warehouse basement—facing Will's family. I wondered who would be tasked with delivering the news that he was dead. And that it was my fault.

The suspect I'd chased down here was crouched over me, his face buried in the crook of my neck. Mewling, sucking noises filled my ears. Terror punched my heart until it felt like it would burst. My hand trembled around the gun pressed into the man's stomach. I'd already squeezed off a dozen rounds, but I didn't have the strength to empty the magazine. I'd lost too much blood.

I could hardly keep my eyes open, but every time they refocused, I found myself looking at Will. In the moonlight slipping through the dusty basement windows, I almost couldn't tell that it was blood oozing from his lips and spreading in a puddle under his face. I tried to pretend that we were back at the precinct. That he'd fallen asleep at his desk again. Maybe it was just drool. I'd give him hell when he woke up, and he'd joke for the hundredth time that he needed all the beauty sleep he could get, and that a young punk like me would know what he was talking about soon enough…

But I'd never know, because I was dying. I'd been so eager to prove myself worthy of the vice squad, and now I would be nothing more than a cautionary tale to warn rookie detectives who got too big for their badges.

Humiliation overpowered my pain, and I found the strength to squeeze off one last round. The creep gnawing on me barely grunted at my effort. *Meth? PCP? Bath salts?* It was the only explanation my aching brain could come up with. Human trafficking *and* drugs. God, this could have been a career-making bust. A massive launch pad for me, and a grand finale for Will. That's what had been on my mind when I saw a flash of movement through the basement window. And look where it had gotten me.

We'd been staking out the building all week. A lucky arrest had turned up a tip about a prostitution ring responsible for the recent surge of missing teens around the city. Will and I had parked our unmarked car in a dark alleyway between two buildings across the street. There was scarcely enough room to open our doors, but after four fruitless nights before this one, it seemed pretty clear that whoever was in charge had been tipped off and had abandoned the place.

It was almost five in the morning. We were arguing about where to have breakfast when movement caught my eye. It was a stray dog, sniffing around the building's foundation. That's when I saw something flicker through a window, something shiny, reflecting the moonlight as it moved around the basement.

I was out of the car with my gun in hand before I knew what I was doing. Will hissed at me to wait, to get back in the car. He said that we needed to call for backup. But my feet moved on their own. There were young girls being held captive, and we were going to find them. I was sure of it.

The only thing I was sure of now, with a drug-addicted cannibal at my throat, was that I was a reckless idiot.

A soft whimper drew my attention to a spot across the room, and for a moment, I could have sworn I saw a dog lurking in the corner. I was hallucinating. *Great.* At least that meant I wouldn't have to endure this agony much longer. I was ready for my life to flash before my eyes and be done with this nightmare. I thought back as far as I could, trying to jumpstart the event.

One of my earliest memories took place under a kitchen table. A pink, plastic stethoscope dangling between my blond pigtails, the business end pressed to the chest of my mother's first partner, a beautiful German Shepherd named Maggie.

My mother, Toni Skye, was what the department called a natural-born hero. She'd worked her way up from patrol to the K9 unit, and then she'd transferred to vice after we lost Maggie.

Maggie had been my favorite patient. *Doctors are not supposed to have favorites,* I'd tell her at every appointment, but I knew she wouldn't report me to the medical board.

The memory pulled one corner of my mouth up in a lazy grin, even as the life drained from my body, and my skin grew cold and clammy. My muscles slowly unclenched. I couldn't feel the gun in my hand anymore. I couldn't even feel the teeth in my throat, though I could hear them working me over, a horrid gnashing sound that echoed in my skull.

And then I saw her—a flash of dark fur darting through the moonlight. *Maggie?* Had she come to deliver me from evil?

My vision warped, eyelids fluttering their last as I began to lose consciousness. I strained to keep them open, waiting to see if my mother would show next. She always arrived a moment behind Maggie. Why should it be any different in the afterlife?

As if answering my silent request, the silhouette of a woman rose up before me, towering over the brute at my neck. My eyes watered as they rolled back in my head, and my heart strummed out a hopeful staccato.

Then, it stopped.

Chapter Two

As a St. Louis cop, I was no stranger to the county morgue. Of course, I'd never seen it from this particular angle. Or while wearing less than a co-ed on spring break.

Goosebumps spread from my shoulder blades to my ass, picking up again at my calves, all pressed against an ice-cold metal table positioned under an overhead light. My tongue felt like sandpaper against the roof of my mouth, my muscles concrete encasing rebar bones. If I were dead, then this was surely rigor mortis.

The pong of ammonia and disinfectant permeated the air, and as my focus sharpened, I heard a trickle of music cut through the ringing in my ears.

"Don't tell my heart, my achy, breaky heart," someone sang along. I prayed for God to strike them dead.

When my prayer went unanswered, I turned to get a better view of hell. That's what this had to be. It was the very spot where my life had ended. The first time, anyway.

I counted the cold chambers stacked against the wall to my left. Two down and three across. That's where my mother's body had remained until her autopsy was finished, and my sister and I were allowed to bury her. That was the last time I'd seen either of them.

The music and the grating voice grew louder. I twisted

my head to the right and found Vin Hart, the morgue's new forensic pathologist, pulling on a pair of blue gloves. His eyebrows lifted, and he scrunched his face a few times as if trying to encourage his glasses to move farther up the bridge of his nose. Then he picked up a scalpel from a metal cart and turned toward me.

"Vini, Vidi, Vici," I croaked, the high school nickname sounding less teasing and more like a plea coming from my dry throat.

Vin squealed—a full-on, being-eaten-alive-by-a-giant-tarantula squeal. He stumbled backward, knocking over the metal cart and scattering his horror film arsenal across the linoleum floor. Then he squealed again and tried to climb up onto the counter that spanned the wall behind him, dislodging a desk lamp and the small clock radio crooning suicidal country music. Because, apparently, this place wasn't depressing enough.

The scalpel was still clutched in Vin's gloved hand. He pointed it at me as I moaned and sat upright on the autopsy table. My muscles and tendons protested, cramping agonizingly under my skin. I tried to stretch my neck from side to side, but that only made things worse.

"Y-y-you're dead!" Vin shrieked.

I glared at him and covered my breasts with my arms. "Where are my clothes?"

He squinted at me as if I'd asked a trick question. "I…uh… I had to cut them off. They were covered in blood anyway. You wouldn't want them."

I cocked an eyebrow. "Well, Pervy McPervertson, think you could find something else for me to wear?"

"You didn't have a pulse. I swear!" Vin held up a gloved finger with his free hand. "This is not my fault. They delivered you in a body bag and everything."

With all the bizarre questions rattling around in my head, clothes should have been the least of my worries. But interrogations were hard enough when dressed. Nudity took things to a whole new level.

I stared at Vin, watching his mental wheels turn as his pupils constricted until I could once again see the milk chocolate color of his irises. He glanced down at his hand holding the scalpel and quickly discarded the blade on the counter before peeling off his gloves.

"I have some gym sweats in my car," he said, easing his way around the perimeter of the room. It was as if he expected me to give chase. And here I thought our high school feud had zapped that delusion.

Vin cleared his throat when he reached the exit. "Uh, I'll be right back. Don't go anywhere," he added, closing the door behind him.

"Right." I snorted and hugged my chest tighter as a shiver

shook my shoulders.

There was a sour pit in my stomach, and it felt as if it were burning right through to my navel as I desperately tried not to think about the fact that Vin Hart had cut off my clothes while I lay unconscious on a metal table in a morgue. Nope. Nothing creepy about *that*.

The room felt as if it were spinning around me. Slowly at first, but gaining momentum as I tried to recall how I'd ended up here. The basement, the crazed suspect, the dog… Will. The dots were all there. I just couldn't connect them into anything that made sense. I closed my eyes and pressed a hand to my face, trying to swallow the bile building in the back of my throat.

Something thudded against the door, and Vin's clumsy return snapped my attention back to the here and now. His sneakers squeaked on the floor as he inched toward me, digging his hand down into a gray duffle bag.

"Here." He tossed a wadded bundle of clothes into my lap from a safe distance away.

"Thanks," I said, before realizing the clothes were damp from his most recent workout.

"I'm so sorry, Jenna." Vin's eyes welled, and he turned his back without me having to ask.

"Don't sweat it," I said, making a face at the ragged sweatpants he'd loaned me. I stuffed my shaky legs into them before easing off the table and jerking them up my thighs. They were too big, but I managed to tighten the drawstring enough until the waistband stayed around my hips.

"I really am." Vin sniffled. "I swear, you didn't have a pulse. This is incredible. We need to call Captain Mathis—"

"I'll call him later," I said, yanking his pit-stained tee shirt over my head. "I want a hot shower and some food first. Maybe a nap."

Vin ran a hand through his dark hair and let out a nervous laugh. "You've been in a locker since six this morning." He glanced down at his watch. "That's fourteen hours, Jenna. Can you imagine if you'd woken up in there?"

I tried to remember what time Will and I had stormed the warehouse. *Will.*

"Where's my partner?" I asked, my eyes migrating back toward the cold chambers.

"Your partner?" Vin stole a glance over his shoulder before deciding it was safe to look at me.

"Detective Will Banks?"

"Oh." His eyes drooped at the corners as he pushed his glasses up his nose. "He didn't make it. I'm sorry."

"Which one?" I took a step toward the cold chambers, trying to read the names on the doors. I spotted my own and swallowed. *Fourteen hours.* How was that possible?

"Are you sure you want to do this right now? I mean,

after everything you've—"

"Which one?" I repeated, taking another step forward.

"Here." Vin circled the autopsy table and gave me a sidelong glance before he grasped the lever of a door next to my vacated chamber. At least I'd been in good company.

The table slid out of its cubby with a sigh. And then Vin folded the sheet back, revealing Will's ashen face and the swell of his shoulders. I begged my heart to turn to stone. I'd have myself a long, hard cry later, but not here. Not in front of Vin or over Will's body. He deserved better than that from me. I thought of his family.

"His wife…" I said, a lump welling in my throat before I could finish the question.

"She was here this morning," Vin said. "With their daughter."

I belonged in hell. It should have been Will who survived the basement. Not me. It had been my dumb mistake. And I didn't have anyone waiting at home. No one depended on me. Hell, I didn't even have a house cat to complain about my absence.

A blossom of old scar tissue was nestled below Will's exposed collarbone. He'd been shot there while making a drug bust with my mother. I remembered visiting him in the hospital the week before my high school graduation.

"You're smart for going to critter school, Jen," he'd said to me,

his thumb hovering over a morphine pump grasped in his free hand. *"At least you'll know when you're working with an animal."* I should have heeded his warning and stayed in the vet program. But when my mother died later that year, I buried my dreams with her.

I pressed a finger to the mound of scar tissue and heard Vin suck in a soft breath. A lecture about not touching evidence was winding up. I could feel it. But Will wasn't evidence. He was a lifeline that had kept my mother's memory alive. That had kept me grounded once she was gone.

My eyes trailed away from the familiar scar and up to Will's neck. A jagged gash ran from behind his ear to the hollow of his throat. The skin had been folded back and in on itself, but I could see the depth of the wound where it gaped open here and there. My stomach roiled, and my hand went to my throat, feeling for the damage I knew I'd sustained.

But there was nothing. Not even a scratch. My skin was perfectly intact and as cool and smooth as marble. That couldn't be right. I covered my mouth and tried to think. Nothing made sense right now, and I couldn't decide if I was delusional or just dehydrated. *I need some water*, I thought as my tongue scraped the roof of my mouth again.

"What'd you put down on your initial report for my COD?"

"Uh." Vin cleared his throat. "I couldn't find any injuries, despite the fact that you were covered in blood. I was thinking aneurysm or stroke perhaps." I snorted, and his ears turned bright pink. "The autopsy would have been more conclusive. Obviously, that won't be needed now."

"An aneurysm?" I folded my arms as Vin replaced the sheet over Will's face and slid him back inside the cold chamber.

"I don't know." He took a deep breath and frowned thoughtfully. "Maybe you saw the assault on Detective Banks, went into shock…and had a nosebleed?"

"And it hit pause on my pulse for fourteen hours?"

"It's nothing short of a miracle." Vin nodded, agreeing with my sarcastic assessment. "You should really be checked out by your regular MD. I've already gathered any evidence from, uh…your person—" He paused to clear his throat again, and his face flushed. "There were no defensive wounds. No signs of rape—"

"Make me a copy of the report," I snapped. The air in my lungs burned. My hand migrated back up to my neck. Something was missing. This wasn't right. I needed to go back to the scene.

Vin's face creased. "I'll have to clear it with Captain Mathis first. That's classified information for a case you're not assigned to."

"Excuse me?" I ground my teeth together as I stared him

down. "You just stripped me naked and poked and prodded my unconscious body, and you wanna tell me your findings are *classified?*"

He took a step back. "I'm really sorry, Jenna, but it's protocol. I can call Captain Mathis now if you want. I'm sure he'll approve the request right away."

"Forget it. I'll read the report when I head into the office in the morning. You know, before I file a sexual assault claim."

"Jenna." His face crumpled, and he gave me a wounded scowl. "Don't say that. I feel horrible enough as it is."

"Yeah, I could really tell how broken up you and Billy Ray were when I came to."

"Music helps me focus. It gets lonely down here by myself." His eyes glossed over, and despite my building fury, guilt slugged me in the gut. I took a deep breath. And then another.

"I guess my gun and badge have already been taken into evidence?"

Vin nodded. "Your wallet and everything else, too. We really should call the captain—"

"I swear to God, if you try to lecture me on protocol again, I'm going to stuff you into one of these cold lockers."

His lips snapped shut. "Got it."

"Can I borrow a few bucks for a taxi?" I gave him a tight

smile. Following my threat, the sudden request probably made me look like a schoolyard bully after his lunch money. "I'll pay you back," I added when he hesitated.

Vin untied his scrubs and began stripping them off. "I can drive you home."

"Great. Let's go." I tugged the sweatpants up higher on my hips and made for the exit.

"But how are you going to get inside without your keys?" he called after me.

"Let me worry about that one, Vin." I held the door open and waved my arm to hurry him along.

Vin drove a rust-spotted, lime-green Volkswagen Beetle. It was a classic model that came with all the classic problems. The thing lumbered like a dying bear through Friday night traffic down I-170, making what should have been a fifteen-minute drive to my house take closer to thirty minutes.

I sank into my seat as a semi blared its horn and moved into the next lane over to pass us. The streetlights and headlights and flashing billboards made my eyeballs feel like they were boiling in their sockets. I tried to roll the window down to get some fresh air, but the lever came off in my hand.

"Sorry, I've been meaning to get that fixed." Vin gave me

a nervous smile and cleared his throat for the fifth time. "The radio works fine, though, if you'd like—"

"If I die in this Nazi deathtrap, it will not be to the sounds of Waylon and Willie." I propped my elbow on the windowsill of the door and covered my eyes with my hand. Maybe feigning sleep would keep him from dragging the conversation down memory lane. That's where I always ended up with Vin. He couldn't help himself.

"So, are you going to the reunion in August?" he asked, drawing an immediate groan from me.

"No."

"Why not? You're one of the most successful graduates from our class."

I snorted. "Says the guy with a doctorate."

"Says the guy who carves up dead bodies for a living," he grumbled. "Trust me, hunting down bad guys is way more impressive."

"Oh, yeah?" I pulled my hand away from my face and scowled at him. "Think everyone will think it impressive when they find out that I got a nosebleed and passed out while my partner was being murdered ten feet away?"

Vin swallowed, and his hands tightened on the steering wheel. "You don't know that's what happened, and you won't know until you get a proper physical."

I resumed glaring out the window.

We finally exited off the highway and headed east on Olive Boulevard. I breathed a little easier then. My precinct was in the opposite direction. Vin's persistence that we should contact the captain had me worried that he might deliver me to his doorstep straightaway.

I wasn't ready to face Mathis. I needed time to collect myself and remember something useful to the case. Without that, all we'd have to talk about is what a complete and utter failure I was as a detective. How I'd rushed in without backup and gotten my partner killed, all in my first week on the vice squad.

My throat swelled every time thoughts of Will entered my mind. God, what was I going to tell Alicia and Serena? They'd expect answers from me, even more so than the captain would. Even more than the local news hounds, who would undoubtedly come knocking for a statement—about my partner's fate *and* my peculiar resurrection. I didn't have answers for anyone. Not even for myself.

Vin's hand squeezed mine unexpectedly, and I jumped.

"What?" I blinked a few times to keep my tears in check before glancing up at him.

"We're here," he answered slowly. His mouth opened as if he wanted to say more but feared I might chew his face off.

I pulled my hand away. "Thanks for the ride. I'll return your clothes tomorrow."

"Keep them," he said, giving me a lopsided grin. If he expected me to swoon over skunky gym sweats, he was dumber than he looked.

"Okay, then." I pushed the passenger door open, cuing a gasp from Vin.

"Let me get that for you," he said, opening his own door.

"I've got it." I scrambled out of the car as fast as my aching body would allow and slammed the door behind me. "Thanks again," I said over my shoulder as I headed up the front lawn. The grass was dewy on my bare feet, and it glistened in the yellow glow of my porch light.

"Don't forget to call your doctor in the morning and make an appointment," Vin shouted to me. He stood in the fold of his open door, one arm resting on the roof of the Beetle.

"Yup."

"And don't forget to call the captain, too. Soon," he added.

I gave him a half-hearted salute from my front porch, hoping it would prompt him to get back into his car and leave. I really didn't want him to know where I kept my hide-a-key. Of course, if he tried to use the thing, I'd have a perfectly legitimate reason to kick his ass—something I'd fantasized about since high school.

Vin's brow creased as he stood there watching me. When

it became apparent that he wasn't going to leave until I was safely inside, I huffed and stepped off the porch.

The mulch in the front flowerbed stuck to the bottom of my feet as I made my way to the flower box under my bedroom window. I stuffed my hand down behind a cluster of morning glories and dug around in the dirt until I found the faux rock with my spare key hidden inside. Not the cleverest of tricks, but it hadn't failed me yet. I hurried back to the porch and unlocked the deadbolt on the front door.

"Goodnight," Vin called as soon as had I stepped inside.

I threw my hand up, sparing him a quick wave before slamming the door shut behind me. I pressed my back against the living room wall and breathed in the cool air. It smelled like oranges and vanilla. It smelled like my mother.

My eyes brimmed with tears as Vin's headlights flashed through the window. I was finally alone with my grief, and it came for me with a vengeance. I slid to the hardwood floor and sobbed myself into hysterics in record time. Misery and I were old friends.

Before I graduated from the police academy, I'd been required to see a shrink. They wanted to make sure my head was in the right place since my mother had died only two years before. I think they expected me to have a chip on my shoulder. A score to settle. But that wasn't what I was doing there. I wasn't some crazy, orphaned girl with a vendetta.

Toni Skye hadn't just been a hero in the department. She'd been *my* hero. My childhood dream of becoming a veterinarian had been born out of a desire to someday work with her on the K9 unit. I was a timid, tiny girl who loved her mommy. I was terrified of guns, and Disney villains gave me nightmares—especially Cruella De Vil. I didn't want to be a cop. But I loved animals. Well, mostly Maggie. She had been enough to plant the seed.

I didn't find the strength to follow in my mother's footsteps until after she was gone. It felt as if it were the only way to be close to her, to keep her memory alive. This was my way of honoring her.

The academy shrink didn't think so. She said I was having trouble letting go, but that was better than wanting an excuse to rough up suspects in some screwball quest for blind justice. So she'd cleared me. Her final word of advice had been that I should take some time to grieve properly. I'd had about all the grieving I could stomach. And there was nothing proper about it.

When my sniveling hiccups finally tapered off, I pulled myself off the floor and clicked on the lamp in the corner of the living room. My mind was already in recovery mode. I was well-accustomed to this process. Step one: cry face off. Step two: drink a gallon of water. Step three eluded me as I rounded the corner and clicked on the kitchen light.

A half-eaten sandwich and bag of potato chips had been left open on the counter. Right next to my bloody house keys.

Chapter Three

I stood frozen for a long moment, staring at the bloody keys on my kitchen counter. They had been in my pocket last night. I remembered stuffing them in there with a handful of mints I'd swiped from Will's desk before we left the precinct. They should have been in evidence with everything else that had been on me when my body was found. What the *hell* were they doing here?

The sandwich and chips were alarming, too. My memory was a bit scrambled, but I wasn't one to leave food lying around for the bugs to snack on. Someone had been here. Someone was *still* here, I realized as my ears pricked at the sound of creaking floorboards behind me.

I ducked just in time. A baseball bat whooshed over my head. As I spun around to get a visual of my attacker, a foot landed in the center of my chest, sending me backward over the counter. The chips and sandwich went flying. My hand slapped out to brace my fall, and I managed to snag my bundle of keys before flipping ass over elbows and landing in a mangled heap on the floor.

I hurled the keys over the counter, trying to buy myself time as I scrambled to my feet and into the pantry where I kept a spare .380 hidden in a breadbox on the top shelf. When I spun around and took aim at the intruder, my breath caught in my throat.

The girl was a hundred pounds tops, all razor-sharp bones under flushed skin. Her tangle of brown hair was wet and dripping onto the collar of one of my mother's terrycloth bathrobes. The bat shook in her hands, and her eyes darted back and forth between the gun and my face.

"*Shit, shit, shit,*" she chanted.

I lowered the gun an inch but kept it trained on her. "What are you doing in my house?"

"You were dead." She gave me a twitchy, nervous shrug. "I didn't think you'd mind."

"So you stole my keys and decided to help yourself to my amenities?" I was beside myself. What kind of person took keys off a presumably dead body? Wait— "You were at the warehouse." I lifted my gun again as a knot tightened in my chest.

The girl shifted her weight from foot to foot as if preparing to bolt. "Hey, I tried to help. I was just…too late. Or so I thought," she added under her breath. Her gaze slid down to my neck.

"What happened down there? What did you see?" I squeezed the grip of my gun tighter to keep my hands from trembling.

"Nothing! Okay?" She blew out a disgruntled sigh and tilted the bat back to rest over one shoulder. "Your secret's safe with me."

"Secret?" Nausea stirred in my stomach. Maybe I didn't want to know what had happened in the basement. What if I'd done something even worse than watch my partner die?

I swallowed and panted my next few breaths while my vision clouded over, washing the room and the strange girl in shades of red. That was new. Something was definitely wrong with me. Vin was right. I needed to schedule an appointment with my doctor.

The girl squinted at me. "Oh, man. You don't know. Do you?" She took a tentative step toward me, her hands wringing the neck of the bat.

"Get back!" I shook the gun at her, determined to hold my ground. "I'm… I'm—" *Placing you under arrest for breaking and entering.* The words were there, but my train of thought had barreled ahead before I could get them out.

If I turned her in, I wouldn't be the one interrogating her about what had happened at the warehouse. I wouldn't be allowed anywhere near the investigation—not now that my partner was dead and I'd spent the day in the morgue. I'd be required to take a few weeks of leave and go through a dozen therapy sessions before Mathis even *considered* giving me another case.

Someone else had probably already taken over the investigation. They'd be interviewing *me* soon, and I didn't have half a clue what to tell them. I needed to find out more first, and this girl was the only lead I had. But calling her sudden appearance luck was premature, especially considering she'd made herself a little too at home for my liking.

"What were you doing in that basement?" I asked, trying to keep the panic out of my tone.

The girl sucked on her bottom lip and lowered the bat to the kitchen counter before sliding onto one of the barstools. "Probably the same thing you were."

"And what is it you think I was doing?"

"Looking for those missing girls." Her eyes met mine for a brief second, and then she looked down at her hands. "I promised I'd come back and bust them out."

I recognized her now, from a photograph in the file. It had been dated, taken when she was in foster care. Maybe eighth grade. "Amanda?"

"Mandy," she said, giving me an offended sneer. "Mandy Starsgard."

"Are you homeless?" I asked, deciding I could forgive her for breaking in if that were the case.

She glanced around the kitchen and cocked an eyebrow. "Not at the moment."

"Well, Mandy," I said, finally lowering my gun to my side. "I'm going to need you to tell me everything you know. Who runs this prostitution ring? Where are their headquarters and other locations of operation? Do you think you could identify them and their affiliates from a suspect lineup?"

Mandy let out a hiccup of a laugh and grinned at me. "You don't give up, do you? Not even death stands in this one's way."

"I had an aneurysm," I said, blushing at the absurdity of Vin's theory. "Or something like that. It's nothing, and I'm sure my doctor will agree tomorrow."

"I wouldn't be too quick to check in with your doc." The amusement faded from Mandy's expression. "The humans can be problematic and draw a lot of unwanted attention from the higher-ups."

And just like that, my hope evaporated. I stared at her, wondering if maybe I should call a psychiatric ward rather than the police. Taking her statement about the warehouse incident seemed a bit futile at this point, but even mentally ill people provided useful tips from time to time.

"Yes, the humans. Such a pain," I said, unable to keep the sardonic tone out of my voice.

Mandy picked a stray potato chip off the counter, one of the few that had survived our introduction, and popped it into her mouth. "You think I'm crazy. That's okay. You'll figure it out soon enough."

I sighed and tucked the .380 into the waistband of my pants. "You can stay here tonight, but tomorrow, I'm taking you to the station so you can give your statement, and then to the woman's shelter."

"I don't need a shelter," Mandy snapped. "I need to find the Scarlett Inn and bust my friends out before it's too late. Girls don't last long in that place, not even the ones they turn."

"The Scarlett Inn? That's what they call it?" I wanted to be excited by the new detail, but my faith in Mandy as a reliable source had been crippled. I couldn't take her seriously now. My focus shifted to the unquenched thirst that had plagued me since waking in the morgue.

I yanked open the refrigerator door and grabbed a bottle of orange Gatorade. Mandy gave me a horrified look as I twisted the lid off.

"This isn't going to end well," she said as I turned the bottle up and chugged.

The liquid burned on my tongue and gums, almost as if it were carbonated. Or half-cut with battery acid. The sensation only worsened as the drink ventured down my throat and sloshed into my empty stomach. It gurgled once, twice, and then I was suddenly a stunt double for the Exorcist. The Gatorade spewed across the room in a wide arc, creating a vomit rainbow over the countertop before sloshing against the back of one of the chairs at the kitchen table.

Mandy had retreated from my trajectory in the nick of

time and pressed herself against the back wall next to the sliding glass door. "Told you so."

I gave her a dirty look. "How could you have possibly known that would happen?" I wiped my chin off with the back of my hand and then coughed up a clot of blood across my knuckles. That wasn't a good sign.

"You need blood," Mandy said, creeping back to her abandoned barstool.

"I hardly see how a transfusion is going to help."

"To drink." She raised both eyebrows and gave me a pointed look. "And don't even think about asking me. I would scrub toilets in a truck stop before opening a vein for a *bloodsucker.*"

"Bloodsucker?" I swallowed and winced at the searing pain in my throat. And I'd thought I was thirsty before. "Maybe I should stick to water." I opened a cabinet and pulled down a glass.

"Water won't be any better. Maybe hold your head over the sink this time?" Mandy suggested.

I ignored her warning and filled my glass at the tap. I meant to take a small sip, but I was so thirsty. Before I could stop myself, I'd downed half the glass, greedily gulping until cool water spilled over my chin. It soothed my tongue and throat. For a few seconds anyway. And then I was choking and gagging up water over the sink like I'd just survived the

Titanic.

"What. The. Hell?" I glared accusingly at Mandy.

"I tried to tell you." She sighed and rested her chin in the palm of one hand. "You're dead, Miss Detective Lady. But don't take my word for it. Have you checked your pulse yet?"

"What?" I shouted at her. I wanted to roll my eyes, but my fingers were already pressed to the side of my neck, searching. It felt like a million years, but I did finally feel a gentle pulse against my fingertips. "Ha! I have a heartbeat. What now, crazy pants?"

She snorted and rapped her knuckles along the counter's edge. "How many beats would you say per minute?"

My fingers went back to my neck, and after a few seconds of waiting, my patience evaporated. "I'm not a damn doctor. I'll schedule a physical tomorrow, and everything will be fine."

"If you do that, House Lilith will sic their agents on you," Mandy said, a serious note creeping into her voice. "I won't help you if they get involved. They kill mutts like me for sport."

"Nothing you say makes any sense!" I screamed at her. I was starting to lose my cool. Not being able to keep anything down and choking up blood probably hadn't helped. I seized the dishtowel hanging off the oven door and wiped my hands and face off while I waited for my temper to dissipate. "You probably have some contagious disease that you've passed on to me—"

"I'm healthy as a horse." Mandy gave me a smug grin. "My digestive tract and heart work fine, but then again, I'm not the walking, talking, bitching undead."

"I've had about enough of this. I'm calling the police." I snatched the phone off the wall cradle beside Mandy, but before I could punch in any numbers, she ripped the entire base free with one hand, leaving a gaping hole in the drywall. The plastic cracked and groaned in her grasp, and the inner workings wheezed out a dying ring.

"You want my help finding those girls, and I want yours," she hissed. "So quit being stupid and get your shit together. We have work to do, and I don't have time to coddle a baby bloodsucker through the change."

I ground my teeth and stared at her until my vision turned red again. My hand went to the .380 in my waistband, but I didn't get a chance to draw it. The doorbell made us both jump, and the heavy pounding that followed sent my lagging heart into overdrive.

"Skye, open this damn door before I kick it in," Captain Mathis shouted from my front porch.

I was going to strangle Vin.

Chapter Four

Mandy's eyes looked like they might fall out of her head. They sparkled, taking on a yellow hue that I quickly convinced myself was a reflection of the overhead light. Mathis continued to beat on the front door, and I had a moment of panic, thinking that he might actually follow through on his threat to kick it in.

I nodded my head toward the hall. "Go hide in my room," I whispered. When Mandy looked like she might refuse, I added, "Unless you'd like to give your statement to the captain?"

She sneered and slid soundlessly off the barstool before making a beeline for my bedroom. I waited for the door to close behind her, then I cut across the living room and flipped the deadbolt on the front door.

"Hold on," I shouted over Mathis's pounding.

Tom Mathis was a beast. He looked like Tom Selleck—if Tom Selleck had been the Hulk and frozen halfway through his transformation. He filled my doorway and almost had to duck as he forced his way inside without an invitation.

"Jesus, Skye. You look like shit," he said by way of greeting, taking in the borrowed sweats dotted with blood and traces of Mandy's stolen dinner. From the way his nose curled up over his thick mustache, I was sure he could smell the vomit and sweat, too. I fingered my hair with one hand, praying I wouldn't find a rogue potato chip, and closed the door behind Mathis.

"Yeah, the morgue might be cheaper, but it's definitely not as effective as a day at the spa." I folded my arms as I turned to face him.

"You should be in the hospital getting checked out," he said, giving me another once-over. "I stood over your body this morning. You weren't breathing. You were pale as a sheet. What the hell were you thinking having Dr. Hart drive you home?"

I sighed and cocked one shoulder. "I'll call my doc in the morning. I was planning to call *you* in the morning, too."

"Oh, really?" he asked. "Thanks. What's a few extra hours of dwelling over getting my newest detective killed, right? And never mind your partner's death. You're the only known witness to his murder, but maybe you don't think his family deserves justice, is that it?"

"Of course, they do." I gasped and felt my fingers dig into my arms. "But I don't remember anything—not anything useful anyway. I was hoping I would by morning." My face was on fire, and I couldn't bring myself to make eye contact with him. I sniffled and blinked away a tear before crossing the room and collapsing into a recliner. My head throbbed, and my eyes burned.

"I'm glad you're alive," Mathis said, his gruff voice only slightly softer. He was pissed, and he had every right to be. "Having you back is better than Christmas. I still can't believe my eyes. But you know how this works. You'll have to give a proper statement."

"I will," I said, nodding slowly. "Who's heading up the investigation? Collins?"

"No." Mathis groaned and took a seat on the end of my sofa. "The FBI sent in one of their vultures. We've been completely taken off the case, effective immediately."

"What? On what grounds?"

"On the grounds that they tracked the crime ring here from Denver." Mathis rested his elbows on his knees and laced his fingers together. "They're bad news. Much worse than we originally thought. I should have never put you and Banks on that case, not for your first week with vice."

"You didn't know. It wasn't your fault." I pulled my knees up beside me and massaged my forehead with my fingertips.

Mathis looked at me a long moment. I'd witnessed how effective his scrutinizing stare could be on suspects, but I never imagined I'd find myself on the receiving end of it.

"If you're going to ask me something, just ask," I said.

"Did you get a good look at the bastard who killed Banks?"

"It was dark." I shook my head, and my eyes unfocused

as my gaze fell to the floor. "I wanna say he was a big guy, but he was so fast, it's hard to know for sure. He might have been on drugs, he…" My hand went to my throat. I had a vivid memory of the pain I'd felt as the man gnawed through flesh and tendons. The slurping, purring noises he'd made in my ear. The rush of hot blood spreading down my neck and soaking the front of my shirt.

"He what?" Mathis prompted me. But I couldn't go on, not without raising a thousand other questions that I didn't know how to answer.

"He was erratic and foaming at the mouth," I said, rubbing my collarbone.

"What else can you remember about him?" Mathis's eyes took me in with skeptical reserve. "Skin color? Hair color?"

"Again, it was dark." I tilted my head to one side and tried to think. "He could have been blond or maybe even a redhead. In the moonlight, his skin looked fairly pale. Definitely Caucasian."

Mathis nodded and smoothed one side of his graying mustache with a thumb. "Your ma used to bring your school drawings in and pin them up in her office. They were pretty good. You still do much of that?"

"Not really," I admitted. "But I know what you're thinking. I'll try, but I can't make any promises."

"Just do your best. If the bastard is still around these

parts, we'll find him."

"What about the FBI?"

Mathis shrugged. "All we have to say to the public is that this guy is wanted for questioning in an ongoing case."

"But it's not *our* case." I lifted an eyebrow.

"Never said it was." Mathis stood up from the sofa. "But who would argue that it's not ongoing?"

Hopeful vengeance blossomed in the pit of my stomach. "We're going to get justice for Banks one way or another."

"*I'm* going to get justice for Banks," Mathis said. A stern line cut across his brow as he looked down at me. "You're going to take a month off and have a few long chats with Dr. Townsend."

I closed my eyes and pressed my head against the back of the recliner. "Ugh."

"You know the drill, Skye. I can't let you come back until you're cleared by the department shrink." His eyebrows drew together as he stole a quick glance around the living room. "Looks like you might have more to talk about than Banks."

"What is that supposed to mean?"

Mathis fingered the blue curtains over the front window and then touched a framed picture on the wall, one of my mother and Maggie. "This room hasn't changed a lick in ten years, Skye."

"And? So? I'm a cop, not an interior decorator."

"Then hire one." He gave me a pitying smile, and it took all my willpower not to snarl at him.

I was not some broken thing that needed fixing. I'd lost my mother. Most people did, eventually, in life. It wasn't some rare or chronic illness that I suffered from. The fact that I hadn't changed much about my childhood home was not proof that I was off my rocker. I didn't know what everyone expected from me. Was I supposed to gut the place and buy all new fixtures and knickknacks so *they* were more comfortable on the rare occasions that they visited? Was my mother's memory really so painful that they wanted to erase it entirely? And they thought *I* was the one with issues. Yeah, right.

I stood and walked Mathis to the front door, ready to be alone with my thoughts. Then I remembered the lanky girl hiding out in my bedroom in my mother's bathrobe. *Shit.*

"Keep me updated on how your doctor's appointment goes," Mathis said as he stepped out onto my porch and turned around to face me.

"Will do."

"You really should have gone to the emergency room," he added, giving me another appraising glare. "Are you sure you don't want me to take you there now?"

I rolled my eyes. "I'm fine. Really. I'd rather wait and see my own doctor than be poked and prodded by a handful of exhausted strangers anyway."

Mathis made a disapproving sound in the back of his throat, but he nodded. "I'll wait until morning to notify the FBI agent heading up the case, and I'll touch base with Dr. Townsend too, let her know you'll be making your first appointment soon." He gave me a sharp look but followed it up by squeezing my shoulder. "I'm glad you're okay, kid."

"Thanks." I gave him a tight smile. I didn't care for patronizing pet names, but considering he'd spent the day assuming I was dead and feeling responsible, I let it slide.

I watched Mathis cut across my lawn and climb into his pickup truck before I shut the front door and flipped the deadbolt back in place. The truck roared to life a moment later, and then the sound of the engine faded into the distance.

I sighed and pressed my back against the wall, wondering how long Mandy would wait in my bedroom if I didn't call her out. I just wanted a few minutes to myself. That was all. But rising from the dead seemed to have used up all my luck for the foreseeable future.

The bedroom door creaked open, and Mandy's voice echoed down the hall. "Coast clear?"

"If I say no, are you going to come out anyway?"

She huffed and slinked around the corner wearing one of my band tee shirts and a pair of yoga pants. "The FBI getting involved is going to complicate things," she said, propping a bony hip against the wall beside me.

"Ya think?"

"And Raphael had brown hair, not blond or red."

"You heard all that?" I frowned at her. "Does this Raphael have a last name? And what do you mean by he *had* brown hair?"

Mandy snorted out a short laugh. "I told you I tried to help, remember? I might have been too late to save your ass, but I definitely took care of his."

I didn't think it was possible, but my throat felt even drier. I tried to swallow and moved my tongue around inside my mouth, hoping to inspire some saliva. "By took care of, you mean…"

Mandy's lips pursed, and she folded her arms. "Well, I didn't jerk him off. What do you think I mean?"

"Vin didn't mention a third body," I said, pressing my palms to my temples where a headache was slowly building. This was getting out of hand. I had to keep reminding myself that she was a basket case whose eyewitness account couldn't be trusted. Next, she'd be telling me I'd been probed by aliens.

"There wasn't a third body," Mandy said, obnoxious pride lighting her eyes. "Because I ate it."

I crinkled my nose and leaned away from her. "You've got some serious issues, girl. I don't know if I'm comfortable letting you stay in my home with screws that loose."

"Says the bloodsucker who refuses to feed." She rolled her eyes. "If anyone's a hazard in this house, it's *you*."

"Again, with the bloodsucker nonsense?" I pushed away from the wall and headed back toward the kitchen.

Maybe I was a glutton for punishment, but I was going to give this beverage dilemma one more go. My thirst was a constant itch in the back of my throat that felt like it was progressively working its way down to my gut, spreading parched desert in its wake. If I didn't solve this problem soon, I was sure I'd crumble into a pile of dust.

"Skye? Is that your name?" Mandy asked, following me around the corner. "I didn't catch it when I checked your license for an address."

"So that's how you found your way here." I harrumphed. "A real pro at this squatting business, aren't you?"

Mandy didn't look ashamed in the least by my accusation. "I do what I have to." She paused at the kitchen table, her hand hovering over the chair covered in my orangey vomit, before thinking better of it and grasping the back of the next chair over.

"My name's Jenna," I said, rinsing my glass at the sink.

"Should I call you Jen?"

I mimicked the look she'd given me for calling her Amanda. "You can call me Detective Skye."

Mandy snorted. "And you can call me the Queen of

England." She made a crude gesture with her hand at her crotch. "Look, I'm not here to cramp your style. I just want to find my friends and set them free, okay? I already took care of your bad guy, so help me take care of mine."

"My bad guy? Raphael the brunette?" I made a face at her as I filled my glass at the sink. Her brows drew together as she watched me.

"You're not a very quick learner, are you?"

"Cheers." I lifted the glass at her before bringing it to my lips. I was more careful this time, taking the tiniest drink possible. I let the small bit of water slosh around my mouth, enjoying the feel of it against my dry tongue and cheeks. Then I swallowed, paying close attention to my body's reaction.

A split second later, I was gasping and heaving over the sink. Blood splattered the stainless steel basin as I hiccupped out a sob. "This isn't fair."

Mandy sighed—a long, grueling breath that suggested she wasn't thrilled about having to witness this any more than I was thrilled about having to experience it. "Do any of your neighbors have a pet cat they let roam the streets at night?" she asked in a flat voice.

"Excuse me?" I gave her an incredulous look.

"It's not caviar, but it will do in a pinch…and I can hunt it down for you." She blushed and cleared her throat as if she'd offered me a favor that was beneath her.

"You're certifiable. You know that?" I wiped my face with the bloody dishtowel and took a deep breath, trying to decide if I could wait until morning or if I should head to the ER now. Maybe they could hook me up to an IV before I keeled over from dehydration.

Mandy tilted her head to one side, and her ear twitched. "Well, aren't you Miss Popular."

Keys jingled at the front door, and a panic sharper than the captain's visit had conjured ripped through my chest.

"Get in the pantry," I hissed, snatching Mandy by the arm and yanking her across the kitchen.

"Wha—" she protested, swatting at my hand.

"Shhhh!" I placed a finger over my mouth and then closed the door softly so as not to make any noise.

The front door opened and closed, and then the sound of bags dropping to the floor and a heavy sob shuddered through the house. I swallowed and stepped into the living room.

"What are you doing here, Laura?" I asked, folding my arms under my breasts.

My twin sister gasped as she spun around to face me, almost falling out of her stilettos. Her red hair lay in a sleek wave over one shoulder, but her makeup streaked down her face, greasy slug trails brought on by a downpour of tears.

"Is this some kind of sick joke?" she said, her voice

trembling with more emotion than I'd ever heard her put forth on the soap opera she starred in.

"The reports of my death were greatly exaggerated," I said, quoting our favorite author—at least, Mark Twain *had* been our favorite author when we were kids. I couldn't imagine Laura reading anything other than tabloids these days. "How's Hollywood?"

"He's fine," Laura snapped. "We're fine." She sniffled and pulled herself up straighter with a deep breath. "Why did Tom Mathis call and tell me you were dead?"

"They thought I was," I said, cringing. "I spent the day in a locker at the morgue."

Laura gasped. "Oh my God." Her hand flew to her chest, and her glossy, blue eyes swelled with fresh tears.

I turned away from her and glanced across the room at the clock on the fireplace mantel. It was nearing midnight. "I've only been awake for a few hours."

"What in the world made them think you were dead?"

"I didn't have a heartbeat," I answered. "I do now, though, so I'm fine." I thought of the nearly nonexistent pulse I'd felt in my neck earlier and licked my chapped lips, wondering what it could mean.

Laura's eyes picked me apart, making a slower assessment than the captain's had but coming to the same useless verdict. "Shouldn't you be at the hospital, sweetie? You look awful."

"Thanks." I snorted and returned her judgy ogling. "You look…picture perfect, as always."

"Right." She let out a ghost of a laugh and fingered the puddled mascara under her eyes. "I look like I belong on a horror set."

A soft growl sounded from her pile of matching pink luggage, and I sucked in a surprised breath when she unearthed a tiny pet carrier. A straw-colored Chihuahua in a blue vest yipped at me through the screen.

"Someone's valium finally wore off," Laura cooed as she unlatched the door.

The Chihuahua jumped over her open hand and did a belly flop on the hardwood, letting out a high-pitched grunt that sounded more like a squeak toy. Then it hopped up and raced for the kitchen, its little toenails skittering along the floor as it lost traction and rounded the corner.

Laura followed it, and I was a step behind. I remembered Mandy just as the pooch made it to the pantry. It yipped and jumped up and down, scratching at the base of the door.

"Do you smell a treat?" Laura cooed, reaching for the doorknob.

"Wait!" I shouted, the word sticking in my throat as a massive black dog emerged from the pantry—the same dog I'd seen in the warehouse basement.

The creature growled at the Chihuahua, cuing the tiny beast to relieve itself on the kitchen floor. And then Laura really did fall out of her stilettos.

Chapter Five

"When did you get a dog?" Laura had to ask the question twice before I snapped out of my trance.

"I… I don't know," I answered, scratching my head.

Laura scooped up the Chihuahua and ripped a few paper towels off the roll hanging under the cabinets. She dropped them over the small puddle her pooch had made, her eyes never leaving the enormous dog standing in the threshold of the pantry.

"What breed is that? Some sort of German Shepherd mix?" she asked, nervously stroking the Chihuahua. The thing had stopped yapping, but it shivered so violently, I feared Laura might drop it.

"I don't know," I answered again. I wasn't sure I knew anything anymore.

Laura gave me a quizzical frown before her gaze pulled back to the pantry. "She kinda looks like Maggie."

I swallowed and nodded, not trusting my voice. The giant dog made a groaning noise, and I could have sworn I saw its eyes roll. At least it had stopped growling. It threw a cautious glare at Laura before darting through the kitchen and down the hallway to my bedroom. Laura blinked after it.

"Did you move into Mom's old bedroom?" she asked, her voice small and guarded.

I hugged myself and licked my bottom lip. "Yeah, it made sense. I haven't touched any of your stuff," I quickly added. "You can stay in our old room if you want to."

Laura's back straightened, but she looked away from me. "I have a hotel reservation."

"But you brought your luggage here," I said with a frown.

Her cheeks flushed, and she let out a little sigh. "I came straight from the airport to check on the house. And it's a good thing I did. What if you really had been dead, and that poor dog was stuck in the pantry all night?" She made a face at me. "And why would you keep it in there? What would Mom say?"

"What would Mom say?" A scornful laugh escaped me. "Like you care. What do you think she would say about you screwing a producer to get a role in a cheesy soap opera?"

Laura's cheeks puffed out. "How dare you! *Henry's Courtroom* has won multiple awards."

"Two," I said, giving her a level glare. "It's won *two* awards, Laura. And one of them was the equivalent of a Raspberry."

"How would you know? I thought you said daytime television was for sad, lonely housewives."

I knew it was only a matter of time before Laura and I would resort to the familiar script. Though I'd hoped it would take longer than this. We hadn't seen each other in almost ten years, and the few phone calls we'd shared were short and often ended in bitter tears and biting insults. For identical twins, we were nothing alike. From Laura's dyed locks to her stiletto heels, she was a complete stranger to me now.

I ran a hand through my tangled hair. "Stay in our old room or stay in a hotel. I don't care. I'm going to bed." I turned to walk out of the kitchen.

"Jenna!"

"What?" I stopped but didn't turn around. Laura was quiet for several seconds, then she sighed.

"I'm really glad you're not dead. I've missed you." She followed it up with a clipped laugh that suggested she wasn't sure why.

"I've missed you, too." My shoulders sagged as I turned around and gave her a sad smile. "It's been a really long day. Let's talk more in the morning, okay? I'll make breakfast."

Her eyes lit up. "Pancakes?" She squeezed the Chihuahua and bounced him in her arms.

I nodded. "Sure. Goodnight."

Laura lifted the Chihuahua's paw and waved it at me. "Say goodnight, Duncan."

I grinned and headed down the hallway to my room. I'd nearly forgotten about the mammoth of a dog, considering I'd half-convinced myself it had been a figment of my dehydrated brain. But when I closed the bedroom door,

Mandy was waiting for me behind it. I gasped and almost fell over backward.

"How the hell did you get in here?" I hissed at her. "And where did that dog come from? Where is it now?" I shot a nervous glance around the room.

"Think real hard," Mandy said, folding her arms across her chest. She was wearing a different outfit, though it was still one of mine.

"I'm not dead. You can stop pilfering through my closet anytime now."

"Nudity doesn't bother me, *Detective Skye*. Would you like me to strip right now?" She lifted the hem of the new band tee shirt and began to pull it up over her stomach.

I reached out to stop her hand. "Quit being such a diva. That last outfit was fine. I don't see why you had to change into this one."

She jerked her hand away from mine and rolled her eyes. "That outfit *was* fine, but I had to leave it in the pantry."

"Girl, you're one odd duck." I scanned the room again, wondering more seriously if the dog had been a delusion. Although, Laura had seen it, too. So if I were nuts, so was she. Unless Laura was also a figment of my imagination. Why not? Nothing else seemed real. I peeked inside my closet and the attached bathroom before kneeling down to look under my bed.

Mandy watched me with a comical expression. "Who's Maggie?" she asked.

I snorted. "You might be coo coo for Cocoa Puffs, but your hearing is off the charts." I pulled myself off the floor and dug through a pile of clothes on top of my dresser. I was ready to shed Vin's loaner sweats and wash the smell of the morgue out of my hair.

"Well?" Mandy asked.

"Maggie was my mother's partner when she was on the K9 unit. She was a German Shepherd."

Mandy huffed and cocked a hip out to one side. "I do *not* look like a German Shepherd."

"I said *Maggie* was a German Shepherd." I turned to make a face at Mandy before fishing a pair of clean underwear out of a drawer. "Maybe your hearing isn't so great, after all."

The band tee shirt she'd been wearing smacked the mirror above my dresser. I spun around, prepared to inform her that she'd breached my generosity quota, but she wasn't headed for my closet. She stood stark naked in front of my closed bedroom door, her face distorted with pain.

A noise that sounded like someone tromping through underbrush filled my room. Mandy fell to the floor. Her mouth and chin pushed out, elongating as she hunched over. Her back bowed, and a line of dark fur shot up from her spine as if she were a life-sized Chia Pet. When she looked up at me, her eyes glowed, a startling yellow against her furry face. Teeth crowded her mouth as her fingers clenched, knuckles splitting through her skin and curling into sharp claws.

Bones. That awful sound was snapping bones, I realized.

My jaw came unhinged. This couldn't be happening. I should have listened to everyone and taken my ass straight to the hospital. I needed a CAT scan. Maybe even a lobotomy. Who knew? Not me. That was for damn sure.

The dog—Mandy—or whatever it was, took a careful step toward me. This up close and personal, I could agree. She was no German Shepherd. The larger head and long legs were more characteristic of a timber wolf, but those weren't native to this area. Although, one had been shot by a hunter in central Missouri a few years back.

The Mandy-wolf-beast took another step closer, and I finally came to my senses, throwing the bundle of clothes I'd gathered at the creature's face before racing for the open bathroom door. Once inside, I slammed the door and backed across the small room until my shoulders hit the window sandwiched between the toilet and bathtub.

I pushed the mini blinds aside and fiddled with the latch on the pane, wondering how difficult it would be to kick the screen out and climb through. Maybe one of my neighbors would see and call a looney wagon to come and pick me up. That was my best bet now.

The sound of scuffing claws drew my attention across the bathroom again. A shadow passed over the small gap under the door. The beast sniffed and let out an impatient whine, and then I heard the crackling, snapping noise again.

The door opened, and my knees trembled as I slid to the bathroom floor. Mandy stood naked in the doorway. She gave me an exhausted glare.

"You didn't stay for the last part of my party trick. *Rude.*"

Chapter Six

"So, I'm a vampire, and you're a werewolf." It didn't matter how many times I said it, the words refused to sink in.

Mandy sat cross-legged on the end of my bed. She'd put clothes on, and had a buffet of food spread in a circle around her. She'd already plowed through half a box of beef jerky, two canned protein shakes, and a whole package of deli turkey. Her head dipped in an exaggerated nod as she tore into a package of string cheese.

"Yup," she said dryly as if it were no big deal. As if she hadn't just shattered the fabric of my reality.

"I'm a vampire…and you're a werewolf," I said under my breath. I rocked back and forth at the head of my bed, my fingers digging into my knees that were pulled up under my chin. "I'm a vampire, and you're a werewolf. I'm a vampire, and you're a werewolf," I chanted. "I'm in an asylum, and you're an orderly."

"Errrn! Try again," Mandy said around a mouthful of cheese as she ripped open another package. "I get that this is a hard truth to swallow, but trust me, it could be much worse. When I was turned, the John who did it left without saying a word. I almost bled to death. If another girl hadn't shown me how to shift and heal my wounds, I would have."

I wanted to feel sorry for her, but I was too busy trying

to decide if she was another patient rather than an orderly. I wondered what kind of drugs they had us on. What could possibly induce delusions this elaborate?

The box of vanilla wafers I'd brought from the kitchen when I ransacked it brushed my foot. My stomach gurgled as I picked them up. Mandy swallowed hard and pressed her palms into the bedspread, dragging herself farther away from me.

"If you're going to get stupid again, I'm sleeping on the couch," she said. "I can't do any more vomit right now."

"I'm starving," I whined.

"Hey, I offered to hunt for you earlier." She shrugged and dusted a crumb off her leg.

"I'm not eating my neighbor's cat." I curled my nose up at her.

"What about that *rat* your sister brought with her? There's some easy pickings."

"Ugh!" I gagged.

Mandy made a serious face. "If that thing tries any funny business, I'll eat it myself."

"I can't… I can't even think about eating a house pet." I panted as my stomach did a summersault. The scary part was, I wasn't sure if it was out of disgust or craving. My body had turned on me in the worst possible way.

Mandy snorted and picked at her fingernails. "Well,

you're not eating me."

"I don't want to eat anyone," I said, my voice rising and then falling as I remembered Laura. Her bags had still been in the living room when I made my mad dash to the kitchen. "I don't want to eat anyone," I hissed again in a low whisper.

Mandy propped her hands on her hips and sighed. "Well, you're going to have to figure something out, and soon. I've heard about baby bloodsuckers who refused to feed. They turned into ravenous animals, like, for real. After a few days, they had to be put down."

That was reassuring.

"How many days are we talking here?" I asked, wrapping my arms around my folded legs and squeezing until my chest ached.

"Three tops." Mandy's lips puckered thoughtfully. "There's a butcher in East St. Louis. He sells cow blood, but not legally, so you can't ask for it in front of other customers." When I narrowed my eyes at her, she added, "I overhead a bloodsucker mention the place."

"Cow blood? Really?" An acidic taste crept up the back of my throat, and I thought I might throw up from the very idea of it.

Mandy leaned across the bed to snatch the box of cookies out of my hand. "It's either that or rabies. Pick your poison."

"I need a shower," I said, uncurling myself and easing off

the bed. I retrieved the clothes I'd thrown at Mandy in her wolfy form and zombie-walked toward the bathroom.

"Make it quick," Mandy called after me. "Sunrise isn't far off."

"Whatever." I sighed and closed the bathroom door behind me.

A shower is a nice, normal thing I can manage, I thought. Plus, if I really was a vampire, wearing sweatpants had to be against the rules. I was sure it was written in stone somewhere. Maybe inside a gothic crypt in some cursed cemetery. Would I have to sleep in a coffin now? I had so many questions, and with Mandy being a *werewolf* and all, her answers were likely limited. But where did that leave me then?

The vampires Mandy knew were either pimps or sleazy customers who frequented a brothel made up of unwilling homeless girls. Not the kind of guys I wanted showing me the ropes. Maybe when I picked up my cow blood takeout, I'd bump into a nice fanged fella who didn't care to munch on people either, and I could ask him where all the decent vamps congregated.

I laughed to myself as I turned on the water in the shower. This was some trip. Maybe I'd wake up soon—preferably in a run-of-the-mill hospital—with Will looking down at me. He'd tell me that the bad guys had given us a run for our money, but we got 'em. I'd gotten my melon mashed a little in the process, but job well done. First case closed on the vice squad. I'd bet we even had some kind of award coming our way.

The new fantasy played out in my aching brain and grounded me as I shampooed and conditioned my hair. The steam filled my lungs, easing the burn in my throat. I didn't try to drink any of the water, though. This moment of reprieve felt too good to risk spoiling.

I was practicing my acceptance speech for the award I was sure Will and I would receive when the shower ran cold. I turned off the water and stepped out onto the bath mat, grabbing a towel from the adjacent shelf built into the wall next to the vanity. The mirror was fogged over. I ran my hand through the condensation and tried to smile at myself.

"Please, please," I said to my imaginary audience. "I'm just a rookie. The real credit goes to Detective Banks. I don't know what I'd do without him—" My voice broke, and the illusion died, wiping the smile from my lips. Two black pupils stared back at me, in a face too pale and gaunt to disregard.

Will was dead. He wasn't coming back. We didn't catch any bad guys. We weren't winning an award.

I'm a vampire. The words finally sank in. Just as the rising sun peeked through the bathroom blinds. It cut three thin lines across my shoulder, searing the flesh like a laser.

"Ow! Shit!" I flinched, stumbling back against the door. I reached for the handle and yanked it open, but before I could go any further, darkness fell, and I was dead to the world.

Chapter Seven

When my eyes peeled open, the alarm clock on my bedside table read 8:20 P.M. *Perfect.* I wondered if Laura would still be in the mood for pancakes. I'd promised her breakfast before accepting my predicament, and now the thought of food made my skin crawl. If Gatorade could make me vomit blood, I didn't want to know what flapjacks were capable of. It was beginning to dawn on me how impossible living a normal life would be.

I sat up and rubbed my face. I didn't remember making it to my bed last night—or putting on clothes. When the tag of my tank top tickled my chest, I realized I must have had help. My first guess was Laura, but she would have called 911 if she'd found me unconscious on the floor. Plus, she would have ditched my original pajama selection for something that actually matched, and she wouldn't have put my tank top on backwards.

The bathroom door opened, shedding light into the dark room. Mandy leaned against the doorframe, her mouth foaming with toothpaste. "Thank *God*," she said. "Your sister is killing me. She's got to go—she and that *thing* she brought with her."

I squinted at her in the harsh light. "Is that my toothbrush?"

"Ew." She made a face at me. "It's a new one I found in the cabinet."

Thinking of teeth, I shoved two fingers into my mouth to touch the tips of my canines, checking them for abnormalities. "Ith I'm a vampire, why don't I hath thangs?" I asked, sounding like a dunce trying to carry on a conversation with a dentist.

Mandy paused her brushing and poked her head out of the bathroom. "They only come out when you feed."

"Really?"

She snorted and spat in the sink. "Hate to burst your blood bubble, but you don't get a cape either. So unfair, I know."

"But sunlight is a definite no." I twisted my arm around and found three black lines cutting across my skin, right under the cap of my shoulder. "Why hasn't this healed, like my neck did?"

Mandy stepped out of the bathroom and took a closer look at my arm. "That's sun damage. It won't heal—not fully."

I groaned. "So beach vacays are out, along with the fine dining. What else should I know?"

"Hmm?" Mandy had dipped back inside the bathroom and was pillaging through my makeup drawer. She held up a tube of peach lipstick and made a gagging noise.

"I know you were looking forward to ransacking my

place, but since I'm alive and all, could you maybe…not?" I said.

She continued her rummaging. "Technically, you're not alive. You're one of the undead."

"I'm alive enough to kick your ass." I tossed the covers back and threw my legs over the side of the bed.

Mandy slammed the drawer and rolled her eyes. "This would be *sooo* much easier if you *had* died. I probably would have found the Scarlett Inn by now and saved everyone."

I gawped at her. "No one's keeping you here. I've been out cold for, what?" I did the math in my head. "Fifteen hours? You could have taken off any time."

Mandy groaned and grasped her hip with one hand. "I couldn't very well leave you naked on the floor for your sister to find, now could I? She would have called an ambulance, and then one of the hospital spies would have alerted House Lilith. They'd send in the cavalry, and when they were done covering up this shit show, there wouldn't be enough of you and me left to interest your sister's rat-faced *Duncan Punkin*." The corners of her mouth twisted downward. "The way she baby talks that thing…it's criminal. Makes me want to eat him out of pity al—"

I held up a hand to shush her. "Back up. House Lilith? That's the second time you've mentioned them. Who are they?"

Mandy tucked a lock of her unruly hair behind her ear and

hugged herself. "They're the vamps that make the rules—around here anyway. They're responsible for keeping our kind safe and in the shadows. If you put a toe out of line, they're the ones who chop it off."

I shuddered. "Do they run this Scarlett Inn?"

"Doubt it." Mandy shrugged. "But then again, I'm not exactly on the up and up with all the latest vamp news. I'm a mutt, so I do my best to stay off their radar."

"A mutt?" The word seemed so degrading.

"I don't have a pack," Mandy said. "Not officially, anyway." She inhaled a soft gasp. "I guess you're sort of a mutt, too, since I ate your sire and all."

My skin crawled at the memory of the creep who had feasted on me. My *sire*. The word felt all wrong. Of course, I didn't think he had intended for me to survive our little encounter.

"How did this happen?" I asked, waving a hand down at myself. "Obviously, it was an accident, but…how—"

Mandy lifted both eyebrows and barked out a laugh. "Dumb luck? Hell if I know. I mean, I'm not exactly a tidy eater—"

"I've noticed."

"So maybe some of Raphael's blood got into your mouth?"

I narrowed my eyes at her. The cop in me was searching for the big money questions now, and I could tell her patience was wearing thin. "How do you know this Raphael?"

Mandy sighed and circled out of the bathroom and around to my closet. I didn't reprimand her this time, hoping the leniency would earn me a few more answers. She knelt down and inspected the shoes on the rack that ran under my hanging clothes.

"Raphael runs the Inn—he and his sister, Scarlett. She's the brains, and he's the muscle. He also breaks in a lot of the girls." Mandy's shoulders squared, and she cleared her throat before going on. "I've never known him to turn one, though. Baby vamps are harder to control than baby wolves, so they have a deal with a local alpha. A free ride for a bite," she said, holding up a pair of battered Converse sneakers.

"Ugh. Why?" Maybe I wasn't acclimated enough to my new condition to think it through on my own, but I couldn't understand the benefit of a harem of unwilling, werewolf prostitutes. From the cold rage in Mandy's eyes as she looked up at me, I wasn't sure I wanted to understand.

"Werewolves heal faster than humans," she said softly, nestling her legs under herself where she sat in my closet. "The vampire clientele like to feed, and the wolves like it rough. Catering to them is a dangerous job, and not one that any of us did willingly. A human brothel wouldn't cut it. Not if they wanted to stay in the shadows."

"How many girls did they have when you escaped?"

Mandy hung her head, letting her hair fall over her eyes.

She rubbed the back of her hand under her nose and took an unsteady breath. "Too many."

It was nearing nine before I worked up the nerve to leave my bedroom and face Laura. I left Mandy to forage in my closet after giving her permission to wear whatever she wanted. How could I deny her anything after what she'd been through? Of course, her abrasive attitude was sure to exhaust my charity soon enough.

The door to my and Laura's old room was closed, but I could hear her cooing to the Chihuahua on the other side. All the lights in the house had been left on, and the television hummed with some celebrity gossip show. It was the most alive the place had felt in a long time, and it made me ache with memories.

Laura's yoga mat was laid out in the middle of the living room floor. So very Hollywood of her. On a normal day, I would have taken a long run around the neighborhood and maybe lifted weights at the gym with one of the officers I used to patrol with. I had a feeling there were no more normal days in my future. I didn't know if working out was even necessary now. Didn't all vampires come equipped with superhuman strength and speed? Or was that another disappointing myth like the cape? I really needed someone who I could ask these things of besides Mandy.

Laura opened the bedroom door and gave an exaggerated gasp as she stepped into the hallway. "Wow, you're actually up. I thought maybe you planned to stay in bed until I left."

"You're leaving?" I asked, the disappointment surprising me as much as it appeared to surprise Laura.

"Eventually," she said, folding her arms above her perfectly flat stomach. The sports bra and matching spandex shorts weren't just for show—though Laura modeled for the brand on occasion. "I tried to wake you earlier, but that *dog* of yours is a heathen. It growled at me every time I opened your door and wouldn't stop until I closed it."

"She was trained to be a guard dog. Sorry about that." I gave her a sheepish grin.

"You might want to check your closet for buried treasure." Laura crinkled her nose.

"I'm sure it's fine." Explaining that Mandy could use the toilet in my bathroom seemed like a bit of a stretch, so I left it at that. If this House Lilith were half as scary as Mandy made them out to be, I didn't want to put Laura in any danger.

Laura's brow furrowed as she glanced down at my backward tank top. "I almost called your boss to come to the rescue, but then I found your note on the kitchen counter about not feeling well—along with the vomit. I don't know why you didn't come tell me yourself."

I shrugged one shoulder. "Didn't want to give you any

cooties if I was coming down with something." Mandy really had been looking out for me. I wondered how many times this particular excuse would cut it. Probably not very many. Man, this was going to get sticky fast.

"I cleaned the kitchen," Laura said, making a face. "The smell was too much, and Duncan kept *licking* at the floor."

"Sorry about that. And thanks," I added, giving her a sincere smile. Cleaning puke wasn't something she was probably accustomed to, having a whole staff of maids at her disposal. "I can still make pancakes if you want," I offered.

"Don't bother." Laura gave me a tight smile. "Really, it's fine. You just had the worst day ever. You don't need to be catering to an uninvited houseguest."

I sighed, feeling like a total jerk. "I'm really feeling much better. Have you eaten dinner? If not pancakes, would you like me to fix something else?"

The telephone in the living room rang out a shrill note, cutting off anything Laura might have said. I was too stunned to answer, considering I only ever received a handful of solicitation calls on the landline. Most of my calls went to my cell—which was in evidence and had likely been turned over to the FBI. I wondered what kind of nightmare reclaiming my stuff would be.

Before the second ring had finished, the answering machine clicked on, and our mother's familiar voice filled the silence. "Freeze! You've reached the Skye residence. We're out saving the world, but we'll get back to you in the nick of time. Give your statement after the beep."

Laura's eyes never left mine, and I was sure the pain in them matched my own. The machine let out a long *beeeep!* and then Vin's nervous voice filtered through the speaker.

"Uh… It's me again. Vin." He cleared his throat. "Dr. Hart. I was just calling to see how you were feeling. And to apologize some more, and to see if there was anything I could bring you—food, alcohol, a shoulder to lean on. Anyway…call me back when you get this. *Please.*"

When he hung up and the answering machine gave its farewell beep, Laura pressed her lips together. "Was that who I think it was?" she asked, her cheeks turning pink.

I nodded. "Vini, Vidi, Vici. I scared him shitless when I woke up in the morgue, and now he's hooked. It's like high school all over again."

Laura took a deep breath through her nose and her back straightened. "Why is Mom's voice still on the answering machine? You realize what that must make people think, don't you?"

I ground my teeth together. "Why should I care what people think? And why should I change the recording? It's still relevant. This *is* the Skye residence. Most people call my cell anyway. The only reason Vin used the landline is because my cell is turned off—" I stopped suddenly, realizing that was far too many excuses for someone who didn't care what anyone thought. From the look on Laura's face, she realized it, too.

"Fine." She nodded as if pacifying a child. "Leave it."

"Tell me you don't miss the sound of Mom's voice," I said, hugging myself to keep from crying.

"Ohhh." Laura sniffled and gave me a cold look. "The nostalgia wore off after the third call. Now it just hurts again. Check your messages." She rolled up her yoga mat and then left the living room, closing herself inside our old bedroom again.

I slumped down in the recliner next to the answering machine. The red light flashed the number nine. I cringed and pressed play. The first two messages were from Vin, apologizing up and down for telling the captain I was alive. He rambled on and on, explaining in detail how it had happened. How the captain had shown up to take another look at my body—and well, it wasn't there. If I didn't have other reasons for hating Vin, I could have almost forgiven him.

The third message was from the FBI agent taking over my case, a man named Roman Knight. He had a deep, commanding voice that very politely requested an audience with me. Soon. The fourth message was from Alicia. I listened to it twice, feeling my heart knot itself up with panic when she said she and Serena would be stopping by to see me tomorrow.

The fifth message was from Vin. Again. This time, he asked if there was anything he could do to apologize. He promised he would do anything for my forgiveness. Something told me he wasn't talking about the slip-up with the captain. *A little late for that one, buddy.*

The sixth message was from the captain, asking about my doctor's appointment—the one I never scheduled, since I'd slept like the dead all day. I vaguely wondered if there were any doctors who saw patients at night. Then I wondered how problematic that would prove when they discovered my abnormal heart rate and wanted to put me in a medical journal.

Something clicked in my brain as I remembered Mandy's warning about involving human doctors, but it escaped me as the seventh message began. "Detective Skye, this is Special Agent Knight. Again. As the only eyewitness to the most recent incident in my investigation, I cannot stress enough the importance of our interview. Please call me back as soon as *humanly* possible."

Goosebumps crawled up my arms. Could he know something? Or did he always say *humanly* with such emphasis? Who was this guy anyway? I added Googling him to my immediate to-do list.

The eighth message was from the department shrink. Laura crept out of our old room in time to overhear it.

"This is Dr. Townsend. I'm calling for Detective Jenna

Skye to confirm her appointment for Monday at three. Please give me a call back if you'd like to meet sooner, dear. Thank you."

There was no sense in writing down the time of my appointment, because as long as it was during daylight hours, I was screwed. I hit delete, and then mashed the button a second time before Vin's final, pathetic message could air.

One catastrophe at a time.

Laura cleared her throat. "Dr. Townsend. Isn't she a psychiatrist?"

"My partner died. She'll have to clear me for duty before I'm allowed back." I didn't want to talk about my mental stability, or Will for that matter. Luckily, Laura didn't either.

"What happened to your arm?" She nodded down at the black lines along my shoulder.

"It's nothing. What sounds good for dinner?" I asked, changing the subject yet again.

Laura shrugged. "I'm on a diet."

"But you were going to eat pancakes this morning?"

"So? That's pancakes." She made a face at me and grasped her hip.

"I'll get you a salad from the Spaghetti Factory then," I said, standing up from the recliner.

Laura's brows knit together. "What's wrong with the Pasta House? It's right around the corner."

"I have a couple errands to run on the other side of the

city. I won't be long." I crossed the room and dug a light jacket out of the coat closet. It would help disguise the fact that I wasn't wearing a bra. If I went back to my bedroom to change, I was sure Mandy would insist on tagging along. Having a missing girl—or a wolf that barely passed for a German Shepherd—in my car didn't seem like a very good way to stay under the radar.

Laura watched me slip on a pair of my mowing shoes, also scavenged from the coat closet, with a disapproving frown. "Did you call a cab?"

I pressed my lips together and wiped my palms down the front of my yoga pants, fending off the sweat before it had a chance to rise. "No. I'm taking the Bronco."

Laura blanched. "You still have that thing?"

"Why not? It runs great," I said, a defensive edge creeping into my voice.

I avoided her glare and checked the jacket's pockets, finding only a handful of quarters, a rubber band, and a half-melted tube of cherry lip balm. I fingered my blond hair back into a messy ponytail with the rubber band, earning an extra sour look from Laura.

"You're begging for split ends," she said.

I ignored her and proceeded to apply the lip balm as if it could somehow make up for my sloppy appearance. I was sure that was at least partially to blame for Laura's horrified expression. She wouldn't be caught dead in yoga pants on a

Saturday night. Not in public anyway. Of course, I'd be caught dead in *everything* from here on out. So why not start with yoga pants?

"Chicken Caesar okay with you?" I asked, slipping the lip balm back into my pocket.

Laura shrugged one shoulder. "Sure." The Chihuahua yipped from the bedroom as if he'd understood the word *chicken*. "Ask for the dressing on the side. It doesn't agree with my Duncan's tummy."

"Got it," I said, refraining from rolling my eyes.

I mentally patted myself on the back as I headed for the garage. That made two encounters with Laura in a row that didn't end with one of us screaming. Maybe there was hope for us yet.

I just wished our happy reunion hadn't taken me dying.

Chapter Eight

I didn't take the Bronco out often. Maybe once every three or four months to blow out the cobwebs and refresh the fuel. A little more often during the summer. Up until a week ago, I had a patrol car that I was cleared to use off-duty. As a probie vice detective, I rode along with Will in his unmarked Charger. He'd been picking me up before our evening stakeouts this past week.

I wasn't really sure where that left me in the transportation department now, but Mathis would figure that out whenever I was cleared to return. There was too much else on my mind to worry about it at the moment.

I pressed the garage door button on the wall and waited for the overhead light to flicker on. Then, I yanked open the middle drawer of the tool cabinet in the corner and rummaged around my mother's mismatched collection of wrenches and screwdrivers until I found what I was looking for.

The Bronco keys were attached to a small foam shark missing half its tail—courtesy of Maggie—and a lumpy ceramic badge that I'd made in grade school. There were separate keys for the ignition, the driver's door, the glove compartment, and the back hatch. They'd been with the crusty beast of a truck for as long as I could remember.

Mom had driven an unmarked car as a detective, so the

Bronco had served as my and Laura's training vehicle. It wasn't much to look at, with its beige and mud-colored paint job and rust-spotted fenders, but it was reliable. The late eighties model came with a removable top that was nice during the summer since the AC smelled like something had died in one of the vents. I didn't have time to mess with it tonight, so I cranked down the window after I'd climbed inside.

The garage light spilled down the length of the driveway and tapered off in the street. It shouldn't have, but it surprised me. The rest of my life would be spent in this darkness. No more sunny days cruising along the back roads with the top off. No more playing on the PD's softball league. The slivers of happiness I clung to were evaporating at an alarming rate.

My breath wheezed past my teeth, a warning sign that a panic attack was in the works. I swallowed hard and took a deep breath through my nose. Then I wrestled a key into the lock of the glove compartment and retrieved the tampon box I kept my emergency cache in—a flashlight, road flare, multi-tool, my mom's old Browning 1911 .380, and a few hundred dollar bills.

There was a first aid kit under the passenger seat, but I was less worried about that walking off. I slipped a hundred in the pocket of my jacket before locking the compartment again. Then I fired up the Bronco and pulled out of the garage.

The short drive to hook onto I-170 took me past the Pasta House. The late crowd was winding down, and a pinch of guilt reminded me that Laura had agreed to eat dinner with me despite the fact that I probably wouldn't return with her food until after ten. I felt like an even bigger ass when I realized that I'd have to lie and tell her that I'd eaten mine on the way home or that I wasn't hungry.

I was so fucking hungry.

The strange red haze that had plagued my vision the night before pulsed at the edges of my sight. I turned my head, half-expecting to find a patrol officer making a traffic stop with their cherries lit up. When I realized it was just a side effect of my new condition, the red hue intensified with my annoyance.

Anger. Hunger. I wondered what else would end up making me see red. I added the question to my growing list as the Bronco grumbled off I-170 and onto I-64. The answer came to me soon enough. Right after I crossed the Poplar Street Bridge and entered East St. Louis. *Fear.*

The homicide rate in East St. Louis was seventeen times the national average. It was a scary place to be during the day, let alone at night. The poverty was ugly and gut-wrenching on this side of the river—like maybe a tornado had ransacked the place and no one could afford to do anything about it. Every other building and boarded-up house ran with spray paint tears. That they weren't all abandoned made it even sadder to witness, and I had to wonder why anyone would stay in such a place. But what the city lacked in luxury, it made up for in drugs and violence.

East St. Louis was not my jurisdiction, and unfortunately, I couldn't have made a difference here. No one trusted the police in these parts, and who could blame them? All the police violence in the news seemed set in neighborhoods like this one. The lack of schools and jobs, and the abundance of drugs and violence, had robbed the community of a good and decent life. Even Will, a well-stacked and foreboding man, thought it was too dangerous on this side of the river. How long could someone like me possibly last here?

Now that I was dead, I didn't have to worry about the shorter life expectancy that came with my little field trip. At least, I didn't think I did. That was another question for the list. Just how dead could a dead girl get?

I scrutinized every shadowy face I spotted on the sidewalk, wondering if one of them might know the answer. And when that got old, I began to guess what they might taste like. The heavyset drunk wrangling a rusty grocery cart with only three wheels made me think cheap wine—Mad Dog 20/20. The thug with the hood of his jacket pulled way down over his face, and his pants dragging on the cracked pavement, was probably more like orange juice and Jäger.

Red spilled across my vision again. I licked my lips, and

my teeth scraped over the top of my tongue. My incisors felt sharper. I needed to get a handle on this new problem of mine. Fast. Before I ended up like one of the ravenous baby vamps Mandy had mentioned.

When I finally pulled up outside the meat shop, I rolled up my window. Through the streaky glass, I watched a man in a stained apron escort a young woman to an El Camino with mismatched doors. The security light on the front of the building made their shadows dance across the dirty street. From the way the man scanned the surrounding area as he gripped the girl's elbow, I guessed that she was a daughter or niece. He paused to tug the sleeve of her jacket up over an exposed shoulder and said something scolding under his breath.

The girl rolled her eyes and gave him a peck on the cheek before climbing inside the El Camino. The car made a grinding noise as it came alive, and hip-hop music boomed over the rattling exhaust. The man in the apron rapped his knuckles on the driver's side window and pointed his finger with a sharp look, signaling the girl to turn down the music. She did. At least until the car had made it half a block away.

The man folded his arms and shook his head as he watched the car disappear a block up the street. When he turned and headed back to the meat shop, I jumped out of the Bronco and ran after him.

"Wait! Are you still open?" I shouted.

He glanced over his shoulder and then did a double take. "No." The bell on the door jangled as he pushed it open, and he flipped the sign in the barred front window to read *Closed*. "Now get on home, girl. Before you cause trouble for the both of us."

"Please, I just need one thing." I licked my lips again, but all the saliva had fled my mouth. "I'll pay you double—triple," I said, pulling the hundred-dollar bill out of my jacket pocket.

The man's mouth flat-lined, then he let out a low, grumbling sigh. "Make it quick." He pushed the door open further and ushered me inside, casting one last look down the dark street before following me.

The inside of the shop wasn't much to look at, but it was clean. The cracked linoleum floor was faded, but I could smell the pine cleaner that'd recently been used on it. A couple of tiles from the drop ceiling didn't match. Neither did the few tables and chairs scattered around the small dining area. A handwritten menu on the wall advertised deli sandwiches and various meat cuts.

The man circled the counter, watching me with skeptical eyes. "What's this one thing you need?"

I grimaced and hoped like hell this was the right shop. "A few pints of blood."

"Don't sell blood." His eyes narrowed, and he placed

both hands on the counter.

The red tinges in my vision throbbed as if sensing the lie. "That's not what I hear."

"What's a nice girl like you want blood for anyhow? Ain't you a little old to be pulling Carrie pranks?"

"Blood sausage. It's my favorite," I said, countering his lie with one of my own. The dry sarcasm in my voice probably wasn't the best idea in the world, but my patience was becoming harder and harder to maintain.

The man stared at me a moment longer, unblinking eyes taking me in with calculated reserve. "You're a cop," he said, the conclusion drawing a sharp hiss and stretching his eyes even wider.

"Not here, and not now." I shook my head. "Right now, I'm just a girl looking to buy some blood." I waved the hundred dollar bill in his face. He snatched it out of my hand and tucked it down into a pocket behind his apron.

"Are you insane?" His eyes darted toward the front window, and then he scowled at me. "Don't be flagging down trouble in my house, girl."

"Then sell me some blood, and I'll be on my way." A pain in the pit of my stomach nearly doubled me over. I closed my eyes and groaned.

"What's wrong with you? Don't be gettin' sick in here. I just cleaned the place." He swore under his breath, and then

I heard a paper bag shake open. "Crazy white girl," he muttered. "Take it and get out."

"Thanks." I sighed the word with a breath of relief. A few pints of blood couldn't run a hundred bucks, but he could keep the change. If this cured what ailed me, it was worth it.

I snagged the paper bag off the counter and hurried out the front door, making a beeline for the Bronco. A trio of thugs smoked weed on the southeast corner across from the shop. The smell of the skunky grass smacked me in the face and made my eyes water. They had to have walked right through here mere seconds ago.

I looked the Bronco over in the pale streetlight as I approached, trying to see if anyone was lingering on the other side, waiting to jump me. My keys were clenched in my free hand, ready to unlock the driver's door the second I reached it.

"Hey, Becky!" someone shouted.

I ignored them and shoved the key into the door's lock, willing my hands to steady. Panic was useless in these situations, but that didn't stop the sweat from springing up along my brow. I nearly yanked the door off the hinges when I swung it open, and I climbed inside so fast that I clipped the side of my head on the frame.

"Hey! Where you goin'? We just wanna talk."

I dropped the bag of blood on the passenger seat and

slammed the truck door behind me, muffling the threatening serenade that was growing louder. The Browning in the glove box came to mind, but I didn't want to make a scene. I had what I'd come for, and now I just wanted to leave in peace.

A crushed beer can smacked the windshield of the Bronco, cuing me to jam a key into the ignition. I stomped on the clutch and fired up the truck before pulling a U-turn in the middle of the street. Something hit the side of the Bronco—likely another can—but I ignored it and accelerated down the empty road.

My eyes flicked up to the rearview mirror as I headed back toward the river and the imaginary line of safety just west of it. The thugs were gone, but not the panic swelling in my chest. If they were members of a gang, they were more than capable of signaling others in the city and putting out a description of me and my ride.

This blood had better be worth it.

I made it to the Old Spaghetti Factory in time to order Laura's salad before they closed. Then I thought of Mandy and wondered how many times Laura had tried to offer her kibble while I was gone. So I added a chicken Alfredo bowl to the order, too.

The plastic sack crowded the passenger seat along with the paper bag from the butcher's shop. They crinkled noisily against each other. I hadn't worked up the nerve to try the blood yet, letting half-assed excuses fill up my headspace instead.

What if it had the same effect as alcohol? Wasn't that like drinking and driving? And what if it was disgusting? Did I really want to spew blood all over the inside of the Bronco? That would be a disaster to clean up—or explain if I got pulled over. What if the blood was diseased? What kind of health risks would that pose for a vampire? By the time I made it to the station, I'd added not wanting to be caught drinking blood on the precinct security cameras to my list. How awkward would that be if the captain asked about it? I somehow doubted that he'd be convinced it was a new fad diet.

The station was locked up at this time of night, but there was a side entrance for after-hours access. Of course, my key was in an evidence box somewhere, so I parked along the south end of the building and waited for a patrol car to deliver a familiar face. It didn't take long. A few minutes later, a white cruiser pulled in beside me.

The passenger window rolled down, and Ronnie Jenkins leaned across the center console to frown up at me. "Skye? What are you doing here? The captain said you'd be on leave for a while."

I nodded. "I am. I just need my backup phone out of my desk, at least until mine is released from evidence."

"Guess you don't have your key then either?" His nose scrunched, drawing up one side of his mouth in a grimace. I shook my head. Jenkins groaned, but he rolled up the window and killed the cruiser's engine. I hopped out of the Bronco and followed him up to the side door.

"Thanks, Ronnie."

"Don't see why you couldn't do this during office hours," he said, fumbling through the nest of keys fastened to an elastic hoop clipped on his belt.

"It was a long day," I offered. Never mind that I'd slept through it.

"I bet." Jenkins sighed and glanced over his shoulder at me. "I was real sorry to hear about Banks. He was a good one."

"Yeah." I shoved my hands into the pockets of my jacket as my breath tightened in my chest and burned my throat.

"Everybody's been wondering how it happened," Jenkins added.

"The captain said I'm supposed to save that story for the FBI."

"Oh, yeah. Of course."

I wasn't up for a fishing expedition tonight. He should have known better, but curiosity gets the best of everyone eventually. It had a grip on me, too.

The mention of Will only reminded me that I needed to figure out what to do about Alicia and Serena's visit tomorrow. Having Laura tell them that I was too busy sleeping wasn't going to cut it. I owed them more than that—but how I would deliver was still hazy in my mind.

As soon as the side door opened, the alarm system chirped out its thirty-second warning. I edged around Jenkins and headed for my desk while he punched in his code.

"I'll just be a second," I said, blinking as my eyes transitioned between the harsh floodlights outside to the dim, red emergency exit lights inside.

"Take your time," Jenkins called after me. "I'm going to use the john and grab a soda from the break room."

I hurried anyway, eager to get home before Laura got fed up with me and decided to catch a red-eye back to L.A. There was also the cow blood to contend with. I needed to suck it up and get the feat over and done with. I wondered if I might be able to choke it down in my bedroom before watching Laura eat her salad.

I pushed the depressing thought from my mind as I dug through my desk drawer and found the cheap flip phone I kept as a backup. The battery was dead, but I'd hook it up to a charger once I got home.

Before I went to find Jenkins in the break room, I made

a detour for Will's desk. There were cameras inside the precinct, too, but they were rarely checked unless something turned up missing. Still, I made my pit stop a fast one, swiping the work journal I knew Will stashed in the back of his file drawer. The notes he kept in there were mostly personal for his own reflection. Anything case-relevant would have been copied over to the main file, but not everything made it into his personal notes. Regardless, I was hoping there would be something useful in there to point me in the right direction.

I stuffed the notebook inside my jacket and wedged it under one arm, not wanting to answer any questions from Jenkins, and slipped down the hallway toward the side exit. A dark silhouette cut across the glass door. The floodlights reflected off the white cruiser outside, creating a stark backdrop.

"I'm all set," I said, before realizing the figure was a hair too tall to be Jenkins. I froze. "Hello?"

"Go ahead," Jenkins' muffled voice called from the bathroom. "I'm going to be a while longer."

And me without my gun. *Shit.*

"Detective Jenna Skye, I presume?"

I blinked until the outline of the man came into focus. "Can I help you?"

He held up a leather wallet, and the red exit light reflected off an FBI badge. "Special Agent Roman Knight. I have some questions for you."

My teeth ground together, and I could hardly suppress a groan. "It's really late. Can this wait until tomorrow maybe? I have dinner in the car, and my sister is at home waiting." I shouldered past him and out onto the sidewalk, not wanting Jenkins to catch the conversation and turn it into gossip fodder.

Agent Knight followed me outside. He turned his back to the floodlight, forcing me to squint up at him. "Are you really so unconcerned about your partner's murderer being brought to justice?" he asked, a scathing bewilderment in his tone.

"Of course, I want justice," I snapped. The act wasn't so hard to pull off. Will's death was fresh in my mind, clouding every thought. But I couldn't tell this agent that Will's killer— that *our* killer—had already been judged. The crime ring responsible was still out there, though, so I used that to fuel my outrage. "You have no idea how badly I want those responsible to pay."

Agent Knight stepped in closer to me, blocking the floodlight. I could see him better now. The expensive suit. The tufts of white hair framing his angular face. The ice-blue eyes framed by dark lashes. With the white hair, I'd expected him to be much older. But his olive skin was smooth, and I could smell wet grass and the cocoa butter of sunblock on him. I breathed it in, feeling the flush of anger dissipate, replaced by something more primitive.

"Please, help me out." He touched my shoulder, sending a shudder through me. "I promise to make it as quick and painless as possible."

Red cut across my vision, and my hunger sucker-punched me in the gut. I swallowed and pulled away from him. "I don't remember much about that night. I hit my head and woke up in the morgue." The words rushed from me in a panic. I needed to get away from him before I did something stupid.

Agent Knight nodded. "I heard. Do you remember how many suspects you encountered in that basement?"

"One." The answer stung. It had only taken *one* unarmed asshole. That he was a vampire didn't offer any consolation, and it wasn't something I could share with Agent Knight. Not if I wanted to make it home tonight and not land myself in a psych ward instead.

"Anything especially identifying about him? Anything unusual?" he pressed. I shrugged and reached for the door handle of the Bronco, but his hand covered mine, keeping me from pulling the door open. "Please."

I huffed out an anxious sigh and dragged my eyes back to his. "I think he might have been on drugs. He was… he was *off* in the eyes. They were dilated, and he was foaming at the mouth."

Agent Knight nodded slowly and inched closer, nearly

pinning me against the Bronco. "Anything else?" His intense blue gaze bore into me as if he were trying to extract the thoughts straight from my head.

The overpowering smell of summer engulfed me again, and I suddenly stopped caring about his breach of my personal space. My eyelids fluttered closed, and I breathed him in, pining for the sun though it had abandoned me less than forty-eight hours ago. I wanted to taste him. I wanted to know the flavor of daylight on my tongue. I was betting it was pure bliss.

"Detective Skye?"

"Hmm?"

"Have you been to see a doctor since your ordeal?"

I opened my eyes and found his face three inches from mine. "Not yet."

"Why not?" he asked, giving me a peculiar look. Something that straddled the line between suspicion and irritation. He glanced down at my jacket and yoga pants and frowned.

"I've been busy," I said, squirming under his scrutiny. "Is that all? I really need to get home."

Agent Knight extended a business card to me, pinched between his index and middle finger. "Call me if you think of anything useful."

I hesitated as my brain began to work again. "You have

my phone in evidence. My badge and everything else that was on me that night, too."

He licked the corner of his mouth and nodded. "And you'll get it all back once this case is closed."

I frowned at him and snatched the business card before jerking open the Bronco's door. Will's notebook slipped from under my arm. It grazed my hip as I climbed into the driver's seat, and I quickly yanked the door closed behind me, hoping Agent Knight hadn't noticed.

He stepped back and tucked his hands down into the pockets of his dress pants as I backed out of my parking spot and merged into traffic. I couldn't decide if he knew more than he was letting on, or if he was extra suspicious of everyone. Either way, it didn't sit well with me. I made a mental note to avoid him.

Especially since I had wanted to take a bite out of him more than I'd wanted anything for as long as I could remember. This couldn't be normal. Not even for a new vampire. Could it?

I eyed the bag of blood in the passenger seat and prayed it would be enough to fill the hole burning through my stomach.

Chapter Nine

It was almost eleven before I made it home. I half expected Laura to be in bed, but the blue light of the television danced through the front curtains as I pulled into the driveway. I grabbed the food and the bag of blood and took a deep breath before heading inside.

I found Laura sitting in the middle of the living room floor, a box of tissues crumbled on the rug beside her. Her shoulders shook with silent sobs, and Duncan whimpered in her lap, his little pink tongue lapping her elbow.

"Sorry I'm so late," I said, not sure it was reason enough for this level of hysterics. I *had* told her I'd be running errands first.

Laura gasped and fumbled with the remote, but she wasn't fast enough. David Steckleman—or Hollywood, as I referred to him—crossed the red carpet in a tacky satin suit. A waif of a model clung to his arm, pausing to cross one overpriced heel in front of the other and pout her lips at photographers. She looked like a baby version of Laura, complete with the cascading red locks and bright blue eyes.

If she were older than twenty, then I was a French poodle. Hollywood was at least sixty. I didn't have anything against May-December romances. As long as they were legal. And didn't involve my sister. Or the dirtbag who had lured her halfway across the country when I'd needed her most.

"He cut me from the show, and now this." Laura hiccupped and shook her head, sending her crimson ponytail over her shoulder to rest against her back. She was still in her sports bra and spandex shorts. "I gave up a franchise movie deal for that pig!"

"You gave up more than that," I said, biting my tongue too late.

"Oh, great." She threw her hands up in the air. "Go ahead, tell me you knew this would happen. I'm sure you're just dying to rub it in."

"I'm sorry, Laura. Really." I held up the sack with her salad and Mandy's pasta in it. "I think I have a bottle of wine that would go well with this."

Laura's cheeks flushed, and she hiccupped again. "You *did* have a bottle of wine. Not anymore." She pulled herself off the floor and swayed as she led the way into the kitchen.

"When did you find out you were cut?" I set the paper bag of blood and Will's notebook down on the breakfast bar so I could strip out of my jacket. My tank top was still on backward, but Laura didn't seem to mind so much after a bottle of wine. I draped the jacket over a barstool and unpacked the salad and pasta.

"It happened last week." Laura sniffled and rubbed the back of her hand under her nose before retrieving a pair of water glasses from a cabinet. My stomach clenched as I watched her fill them at the sink.

"Why didn't you tell me?"

"I couldn't bring myself to tell anyone. It was too embarrassing. It still is." Her brow creased, and fresh tears lined her lashes.

"Well, now you can go after one of those movie roles you want. Right?" I circled the counter and nudged her aside with my hip so I could dig a couple of forks out of a drawer.

Laura's eyes drooped. "I don't even know if any other producers would consider me. Typecasting is a real problem lately. I've been with *Henry's Courtroom* since the very beginning. I made that show. Eight seasons, and David decides my character, the legendary Anastasia van de Velde, is boring audiences and needs a rest. I thought he was gearing up to bring her back in some big way next season."

"The show will totally flop without you. You were the only one on there who could even act," I said, blushing when she turned her surprised eyes on me.

"I *knew* you watched." She smirked and pushed one of the water glasses my way.

"Yeah, well. I've been working nights. What else was I going to watch during the day?"

"Mmhmm."

Standing on the opposite side of the breakfast bar from

me with her elbows resting on the counter and a lazy grin on her face, she looked so much like Mom. I often wondered if Laura had colored her hair red for that reason—and not just because Hollywood had a type. With all the accusations flying around about how hard I was trying to fill our mother's shoes, coloring my hair to match would have been too much.

Laura pried open the lid of her salad and laid it on its top to use as a bowl for her packet of Caesar dressing. Duncan did a little dance at her heels until she deposited a chicken strip in front of him.

"I've been meaning to ask," she said, eyeing the gaping hole in the drywall where the kitchen phone used to be. "What happened there?"

I chewed my bottom lip and gave her a pained smile. "Solicitors?" This lying business was getting old fast. And Laura didn't look convinced.

"Huh." She made a skeptical face.

"I'd better check on Ma—my dog," I said, laying a fork on top of the box of pasta so I could pick up the glass of water in my other hand.

Laura's bottom lip jutted out. "You're not going to eat with me?"

"Uh… I'm not hungry. This is for…the pooch. I'll come back and keep you company, though."

"You really should eat something. You look a little

gangly." She gave me an appraising frown.

"Gangly?" I raised an eyebrow at her. I worked out at the gym, and I could lift more than some of the guys in my department. Gangly was not a word people used to describe me.

Laura gave me a weak smile and loaded her fork with salad. "Bring your dog takeout often?" she asked. "Because I couldn't find kibble anywhere in this house. I left a bowl of Duncan's inside your bedroom door."

I pressed my lips together and gave her a strained smile. "Yeah, I'm out. I'll get some more tomorrow. Thanks."

Laura nodded and stuffed a bite of salad into her mouth as I slipped out of the kitchen and headed down the hallway to my room. I balanced the box of pasta in the crook of my opposite arm long enough to wrangle the doorknob open.

"It's me," I said, clicking on the bedroom light and pulling the door closed behind me.

Mandy poked her head out of the bathroom. Her mousy hair hung in ringlets around her face, and I could tell she'd been playing in my makeup drawer. "Where the hell have you been? You just *left* me here. With that *sister* of yours." She put both hands on her hips and pulled herself up to her full height, which was a few inches shorter than me, even though she was wearing my wedge sandals. She had also changed into a pair of my jeggings and an off-the-shoulder lace blouse. My favorite one. I guess that's what I got for setting her loose in my closet.

"Relax. I went to get blood," I said. "One problem at a time—and that one was the most pressing." The knot in my stomach hadn't released since the meat shop incident, and the red had never fully left the corners of my eyesight.

Mandy sniffed the air. "I think your order got mixed up with someone else's."

"The blood's in the kitchen. This is for you." I handed her the box of pasta, and she snagged it with both hands.

"Yes! I am starving to death." She nodded toward the door. "Feel free to take that bowl of rat food and shove it up your sister's ass for me."

I snorted and set the glass of water down on my night table. "She might be staying longer than I anticipated. She just lost her job."

"Great." Mandy rolled her eyes and flopped down on the edge of my bed. She pulled her legs up and crossed them before nestling the box of pasta in her lap. "We're going to have to figure out some other arrangement then," she said, twirling her fork through the fettuccini until she had a bite the size of a tennis ball.

"What do you mean?"

"I mean, I'm sick of playing Fido. Tell her I'm a foreign exchange student or your live-in housekeeper or something."

I shook my head. "I don't think that's going to work. You don't have an accent, and do you even know *how* to clean a house?" I glanced down at the floor where half of my wardrobe lay in random piles.

"I said *tell* her that. I'm not actually going to clean your damn house."

"Then maybe you could at least try not to destroy it?"

Mandy scoffed and proceeded to shove the enormous bite of pasta into her mouth. I was unsurprised that it fit.

At least we could agree on one count. We definitely needed a better arrangement. I picked up a pair of jeans and folded them before tucking them back inside my dresser.

Mandy was too busy gorging to pay any more attention to what I had to say, so I left, brainstorming ideas on how to convince the brat to clean up after herself. And ideas on how I could introduce her to Laura in human form.

Maybe she could be a dog trainer? No. That wouldn't work, considering she couldn't very well be in the same room as herself in wolf form. Maybe she could be interning with me for the week? But me being on leave wasn't the best way to show a junior officer the ropes. A brilliant idea dawned on me as I stepped into the kitchen—and then the doorbell rang.

Laura glanced up from her salad. "Were you expecting company this late?"

"No." My first thought was that the punks from East St.

Louis had somehow followed me home. I opened the drawer of the china cabinet in the dining room and retrieved the Glock I usually reserved for the range. "Wait here," I said to Laura.

I crept through the living room, staying clear of the front window. The television was playing some late-night talk show, and it disguised the squeak of the floorboards as I edged up next to the door to glance through the peephole.

Vin Hart stood on my front porch. A baby blue polo was buttoned all the way to his throat and tucked into a pair of khaki shorts. He held a bouquet of purple and white flowers under his chin, and an anxious smile stretched across his face. I rolled my eyes and opened the coat closet long enough to discard my gun on the top shelf.

"It's just Vin," I shouted to Laura. "I'll get rid of him," I added, not caring that he'd probably heard me through the door. I flipped the deadbolt and cracked the door open wide enough to poke my head outside. "What do you want?"

Vin blinked at me, his brown, puppy dog eyes turning upward in hurt confusion. "I wanted to see how you were feeling. And to bring you these," he said, angling the flowers at me.

I cocked an eyebrow. "I'm allergic," I lied. "And I'm feeling right as rain." Another lie. "Thanks for stopping by. I really appreciate your concern." The biggest lie of all.

Vin blew out a frustrated sigh and ran one hand through his hair, mussing his geek-chic image. "It's been ten years, Jenna. Are you ever going to forgive me?"

I wedged the door open a bit more so I could lean against the frame and fold my arms. "Forgive you for what, Vin?" If he was going to open old wounds, there was nothing stopping me from poking and prodding them.

Vin tilted his head back and shot a bitter laugh up at the ceiling of the porch. "I was a stupid kid, okay? I didn't start that rumor. But," he injected as if he anticipated that I might cut him off. "I should have put a stop to it. That's on me. And I'm truly sorry."

"That's ancient history, Vin." God, I was an awful liar. But it seemed too petty of a grudge for me to own up to. "I can forgive you without wanting to give you another chance to screw me over."

"Screw you over? Really?" His shoulders slumped, and he gaped at me. "I didn't correct someone when they spoke the truth. That hardly counts as screwing you over."

"The *truth*?" I ground my teeth together. Vin's polo faded to a light purple. "Ten years, and you're still clinging to that delusion?"

He dropped the flowers in a wicker chair without taking his eyes off me. "Ten years, and you still deny that the best night of my life ever happened."

"With a hand that good, you should've become a surgeon." My stomach did a summersault, rage and hunger building into a cyclone at my core, and suddenly, Vin was too close. I could smell his cologne, the toothpaste on his breath, his sweat, the musk of his arousal.

"So you do remember how good my hands were," he said, his voice dropping to a hoarse whisper.

I wanted to laugh in his face, but I couldn't catch my breath. Vin mistook my panting for longing. He reached up to touch my face, but I caught his hand. The want in his gaze crumbled into concern when I pressed my nose against the inside of his wrist and took a deep breath. Warm blood pulsed beneath his flesh. I could see it coursing through his veins and arteries, all the more visible in the red hue of my hunger.

"Jenna, you're freezing," Vin hissed. He tugged at his hand, but I couldn't convince my fingers to uncoil from around his wrist. "Your eyes are…are dilated." He gasped as one of my fingernails broke the surface of his skin. "Ouch! Shit, Jenna. What's wrong with you?"

"I'm sorry," I said, finally releasing him. I took a shuddering breath and pressed my lips together, feeling the points of my canines graze the inside of my mouth. That was new.

"Jenna?" Vin took a step back and stumbled down the front steps, landing flat on his ass on the lawn. "Are…are you okay?" I should have been asking *him* that. "You don't look well. Your mouth." He covered his own with one hand, horror lighting up his eyes.

"Thanks for the flowers." I slammed the front door and flipped the deadbolt back in place.

This was a disaster. My hands shook, even clenched into fists and pressed into the void of my shrinking stomach. My skin had taken on a sickly sallow color from the hints I could see, and Vin was right—I was freezing. I pressed my forehead against the closed front door and breathed through my nose, waiting for the nausea twisting my insides to let up.

I couldn't go on like this. Even if the cow blood tasted like pickled livers, I would choke it down if it meant not mauling someone—even a shit like Vin Hart—in my own front yard.

When the red plaguing my vision tapered off to a dull throb in my peripheral, I pushed away from the door and marched toward the kitchen. A plan was forming in the back of my mind. I could take the bag of blood and slip inside the pantry long enough to chug it. Then maybe I wouldn't be compelled to eat my own sister. The thought tightened my throat and sent a shudder through my shoulders. But it was nothing compared to the panic that slapped me once I rounded the corner and stepped into the kitchen.

The paper bag from the butcher's shop lay on the floor.

One of the plastic containers of blood sat on the kitchen counter. The other one was clenched in Laura's hand. The look on her face was a cross between confusion and disgust.

"Is this what I think it is?"

Chapter Ten

I stared at Laura, my mouth hanging open like an idiot, and tried to come up with a simple lie to pacify her. It should have been easy. But I couldn't even get my teeth to stop chattering.

"It's f-f-for a recipe. B-b-blood pudding," I said, wrapping my arms around my middle.

"Oh my God, Jenna." Laura set the blood down and circled the counter. "Are you okay? You're turning blue."

"M-m-maybe the th-thermostat is broken." I caught a whiff of her fruity shampoo, and the salty tears dried to her cheeks. The red eating at the edges of my sight pulsed stronger as she neared me. "Stay back!"

Laura froze, her eyes swelling to the size of silver dollars. "What's going on here?" A line of worry cut across her forehead, and I was sure my expression mirrored hers—though it was likely paler, and I could feel the bones in my face pressing through my skin.

I eyed the containers of blood on the counter, just past my sister, and debated whether or not to risk getting that close to her in order to reach them. But the longer I waited, the harder it would be. And the more danger Laura would be in.

Laura folded her arms and glared at me, the shock and concern quickly shifting into anger. "Are you on drugs? Please tell me you aren't that stupid."

"Not drugs," I said between labored breaths. My fingernails bit into the palms of my hands as I made up my mind. I sidestepped around her and lunged for the blood, taking a container up in my shaking hands. The tacky fluid oozed over the brim as I ripped the lid off and lifted it to my mouth.

A thin film had formed on the top. It stuck to the roof of my mouth, and under normal circumstances, it would have triggered my gag reflex. Not tonight. The blood congealed at the corners of my lips and trickled down my chin, but most of it sloshed to the back of my throat, coating my teeth and tonsils like syrup.

Truthfully, it was gross. Cold and bitter. Not at all what I had expected blood to taste like in my new state of existence. Something instinctual told me that this was not a permanent solution—that it would be like eating stale potato chips day in and day out. It might take the edge off for a short while, but it wouldn't be enough to survive on.

As these thoughts unraveled themselves, I was vaguely aware that Laura was still in the kitchen. Watching me with her hand clamped over her mouth. She made a retching noise in the back of her throat as if she were trying very hard not to barf all over the place. When I'd polished off the first container and set it back down on the counter, she regained her poise. For a second anyway. And then she screamed.

"What. The. Fuck?" She inched backward until she bumped into one of the dining room chairs, and after shoving it aside, she continued her retreat until her back hit the far wall of the room. "That was the nastiest thing I've ever witnessed! Please tell me that wasn't really blood—that this is just some weird prank you're pulling on me."

Mandy appeared in the threshold of the kitchen, brandishing her fork like a weapon. Duncan joined her a split second later, yipping as if he'd caught an intruder red-handed. Mandy's annoyed glare, along with the pointy end of the fork, darted from me to Laura to the Chihuahua to the drippy container on the counter. When she realized what was going on, she groaned.

Laura hadn't moved from the wall, and her hysterics had only just begun. "Who the hell are you?" she snapped at Mandy.

"Erm…" Mandy shot me an apologetic frown. "Zee new maid?" she said in a cheesy French accent.

I rolled my eyes and flopped down on a barstool. "Yeah, my foreign exchange maid, who doesn't know how to clean houses."

"Hey!" Mandy barked, not in protest at my accusation but rather at Duncan's sudden interest in her toes. "Keep your ball-washer to yourself!" So much for the accent.

I propped an elbow on the counter behind me and ran

my own tongue over the blood sticking to my teeth. "I'm a vampire. She's a werewolf," I said in the same catatonic voice that I'd used the night before.

Mandy pointed the fork at me again. "She make funny joke, *oui*?"

"Oh, stuff it." I waved her off and reached for the second container of blood. "I haven't seen my sister in years. I'm not going to waste any more of this time feeding her lies."

"My secret isn't yours to tell!" Mandy stomped her sandaled foot. "Damn it. You're going to get us all killed."

"Ow!" I glanced back at Laura and caught her rubbing her arm. "It was worth a shot," she said, inspecting the pinch welt. "I guess you've really lost it, huh? And you've convinced some teenage nightmare to help you fuel this wacko fantasy?" She shook her head in disbelief.

I sniffed the second container of blood, less eager to down it now that my hunger had been dampened. "Mandy, could you go ahead and shift real quick so we can get through this stage of the process?"

Mandy grunted and bared her teeth at me. "Oh, yeah, because it's just like snapping my fingers. All tickles and giggles. Not like my insides are ripping themselves apart or anything."

"I'll give you a hundred bucks," I said, deciding that was a bad move the second the words left my mouth. Mandy glowered at me, her chest heaving violently beneath the lace blouse.

"Is that all my suffering is worth?" she hissed. "You think money fixes everything?"

"A thousand then?" I gave her a pleading look. "Otherwise, we'll be here all night trying to convince her." I nodded my head at Laura, who was glaring in our general direction.

"Maybe I don't want her convinced," Mandy said through clenched teeth. "Maybe I like my head right where it is, attached to my body."

"Two thousand. That's my best offer."

"Gah! Fine. But I want cash." Mandy yanked the blouse over her head and threw it at me. I caught it then draped it over my jacket on the barstool, careful not to get blood on anything. She chucked the heels at me next, before stripping off the jeggings.

"What are you doing? Stop!" Laura held her hands up to block Mandy from her line of sight. The girl stood stark naked between the dining table and the breakfast bar. I was suddenly glad that I'd replaced the vertical blinds over the sliding glass door that Maggie had chewed off. Mom had left them like that after Maggie died, unable to bring herself to fix anything the dog had maimed.

Mandy gritted her teeth, and her eyes turned yellow,

wrenching a gasp from Laura. The crackling, popping sound filled the air, and then Mandy hunched over. Fur rippled down her back as her spine lengthened. Duncan yipped and scampered across the hardwood floor to Laura, who had slid down the dining room wall and sat with her legs pulled up to her chest. Tears filled her eyes, and she shook her head as if she couldn't bring herself to accept what she saw.

I dipped a finger into the container of blood and nodded, silently confirming what she was seeing. I didn't want to believe it either, but denial wasn't going to do any of us any good. I needed to accept this and move on. There were missing girls in the city. There was a crime ring responsible for Will's death. There were a million other things I had to figure out how to manage as the newly undead, and I hoped nixing the need to fool my sister would simplify that list.

Three heads are better than one.

Our mother had said that whenever she had called a family meeting. Mandy wasn't exactly family, but if she hadn't stuck around and made it perfectly clear what was happening to me, I probably would have eaten Vin's face off and gnawed on my sister for dessert. A roof, a messy closet, a few thousand dollars, finding her missing friends—these were all things I was happy to give.

Mandy finished her shift and gave me a bored look before turning in a slow circle, as if to say *"Ta-da!"* Her fur was mostly black but it faded to a softer brown along her muzzle, over one eye, down her legs, and at the tip of her tail. She was beautiful.

When Mandy turned toward Laura, Duncan lost it. The tiny pooch growled and then let out a series of yaps that rivaled most smoke alarms. Laura looked as if she'd gone comatose.

"Your dog is a girl," she said in a dazed voice. "I-I mean your girl is a dog."

"Wolf, technically," I replied. "But with that coloring, I think she could probably pass for some sort of German Shepherd mix."

Mandy grumbled a whiny bark in protest, and then she began to shift again. Her fur curled in on itself and disappeared beneath gray flesh that slowly softened to a pale pink. The transition to human seemed to take less time and effort, but she was covered in sweat when she finished, crouched on the floor, her fingers splayed across the hardwood for balance. She reached a hand up to finger her tangled hair and scowled at me.

"I *just* curled that."

"The makeup is gone, too," I informed her. Clearly, the cow blood hadn't been enough to replenish my tact—though some might have argued that I hadn't had much of that to begin with.

Mandy snapped her fingers at me and pointed at the clothes laid over the barstool. I tossed them to her and gave her some privacy by turning my attention to Laura. My sister was shamelessly gaping, but I couldn't blame her. As Mandy dressed herself, Laura's gaze migrated back to me.

"I knew it," she whispered, more to herself than anyone else.

I cocked my head to one side. "You knew what? That I was a vampire?"

"That you'd go and get yourself killed like Mom did." Her eyes gleamed with unshed tears. "I told you becoming a cop was stupid and reckless."

"Hey!" I snapped and stood up from the barstool. "Who the hell are you to judge me for career choices?"

"Being an actress is safe and profitable and respectable," she said, ticking off her reasons on one hand while Duncan cowered under the bend of her knees. "It doesn't involve getting shot at. It doesn't involve *dying*." She covered her face with both hands and heaved a wailing sob through her fingers. "Oh my God. How could you let this happen?"

"I didn't *let* anything happen." My throat tightened as I thought of Will and how helpless I had been to save him. How helpless I had been to save myself. "There are dozens of girls who have been abducted around the city and forced into prostitution. I was trying to save them."

"We're going to save them," Mandy added, comfortable joining the conversation now that she was clothed again.

Laura pinched the bridge of her nose and sniffled. "And I thought I had problems. I guess this explains why you slept all day, and why your pet *werewolf* wouldn't let me into your room."

"It's Mandy," Mandy injected, adjusting the lace blouse over her hips. "And sorry about that." Duncan sniffed at her foot, and she made a face. "But sorry or not, you'd better keep that thing away from me."

"Come here, Duncan." Laura made a kissy noise at the dog and scooped him into her lap before standing up. She kept a hand on the wall behind her, and her knees wobbled precariously as she pulled out a chair at the dining room table. She sat down and nervously stroked Duncan's coat. "What are you going to do?" she asked, looking up at me with pitying eyes.

I sighed and rubbed the blood drying between my thumb and forefinger. "I haven't figured all of that out yet."

"How are you supposed to go back to work?" Laura scratched the side of her head thoughtfully. "How are you supposed to *live*?"

"I don't know," I said, the words coming out harsher than I intended. "I don't know anything yet. I'm working on it." My eyes lingered on the remaining container of blood, and I grabbed it as I reclaimed my barstool.

Mandy put her hands on her hips and sighed. She looked less polished without the curls and makeup, like a mangy teenager who had just rolled out of bed. I was reminded of my brilliant idea as she crossed the kitchen and opened the refrigerator, helping herself to a grape Gatorade after sticking her tongue out at the last orange one.

"You were a foster kid, right?" I asked.

Mandy's brows dropped into a humorless line, and she shot me a warning glare. "What of it?" she said, digging a bag of deli turkey out of the cheese drawer.

"If anyone asks, that's what we'll tell them. You're my foster kid."

She grunted. "I'm eighteen. I don't need another foster mom."

"Well, no one's going to buy that you're 'zee new maid.'" I picked up the container of blood and took a careful drink, avoiding spilling it down my chin this time. The pain in my stomach was now a dull ache. This was what I usually felt like after eating too many tacos. Bloated and hungry at the same time. It wasn't a sensation I wanted to get used to, but what other choice did I have?

Laura made a sickly noise in the back of her throat. "I don't think I can watch you do that," she said, pinching her eyes closed as her shoulders trembled.

"Then don't," I snapped. "It's the only thing I've been able to keep down for the past two days, so I'm not going to apologize for drinking it."

"Maybe you should try the kibble." Mandy smirked at Laura as she stuffed a handful of turkey into her mouth and then washed it down with the Gatorade.

"That kibble is the caviar of dog cuisine. It's what Arnold feeds his dogs." Laura sat up taller and lifted her nose in the air. Leave it to her to get offended about her fancy ass dog food. "Where did you get that?" she asked, nodding at the bloody container in my hand. I'd sucked down almost the whole thing without realizing it.

"A meat shop," I answered, leaving off the minor detail of its location. "It's cow blood."

"Is it…good?" Her nose crinkled, but she managed not to stick her tongue out like Mandy had.

"Not especially, but it's helping."

"Helping?" Her eyebrows shot up, and she clutched Duncan tighter to her bare stomach. "Are you having horrible cravings?" She gasped. "Is that why you told me to stay back? Was I almost a victim of your bloodlust?" Her voice rose an octave, reminding me of one of her hysterical monologues from *Henry's Courtroom*.

"I get hungry, just like I did before I died. And I get cranky when I'm hungry." I didn't really want to go into detail about how afraid I'd been for her, too. She was getting wound up enough all on her own. "My vision goes red when I'm hungry, or angry, or afraid. And I uncontrollably fall asleep when the sun rises. That's about the extent of my vampiric knowledge so far."

"What about whoever bit you?" Laura asked. "Aren't they supposed to tell you all the things or something?"

Mandy choked mid-Gatorade gulp and rasped a throaty and unrecognizable sound at me that I quickly discerned as a plea to zip my lips.

"It was an accident, and they didn't stick around," I said, sugarcoating another sketchy answer.

Laura's lips pursed, and her shoulders squared. "We Skye women seem to have a knack for finding those kinds of winners, don't we?"

The thought had crossed my mind a time or two. Our father had bailed before we were born. My high school crush had humiliated me. And now, Laura's producer/boyfriend had dumped her for a newer model.

"I'll figure it out on my own. I'm good at that," I said. Laura flinched and gave me a wounded pout.

"I couldn't stay. I'm sorry, Jenna." She swallowed and rubbed a hand down her arm. "It was too painful."

"You think I wasn't hurting, too?" I said.

"I just needed a distraction. I needed to not think about

her for a while." Her bottom lip trembled. "And you were practically playing dress up. I think maybe you still are." She glanced around the kitchen and out at the living room that Mathis had pointed out was exactly the same.

My heart clenched in my chest. I wanted to deny her claim, but part of me knew she was right. At least partially. Maybe I'd started this new life while my screws were loose, but I knew what I was doing now. And I was proud of it. Even if it had gotten Will and me killed, what we'd been trying to do was important. It still was.

"What Mom did made a real difference in people's lives," I said, forcing the words past my heartache. "I can understand you wanting a distraction from the pain, but the only way I knew how to fix mine was to pick up where she left off and continue her good work. It made me feel like, if I could do that, then maybe she wasn't really gone."

Laura sniffled and wiped a rogue tear from her cheek. "And it made me feel like I'd already lost the only other person I had in the world." Duncan squirmed in her lap and then lifted his tiny snout and howled a mournful note.

I held my hands out, palms up, and gave her a lopsided smile. "That's obviously not something you have to worry about anymore. I'm pretty much indestructible now, so…" I shrugged a shoulder like it was no big deal. I'd meant for it to make her laugh, so when she burst into tears, I was at a loss.

"Nice going," Mandy whispered harshly from the open refrigerator door.

I slid off my barstool and shooed Duncan out of Laura's lap so I could kneel down and wrap my arms around my sister. "Hey, hey. Don't do that. It's going to be okay. Why are you even crying? I'm fine. I'm *better* than fine."

She tucked her runny nose into my hair while I stroked her back. "You're dead. Oh my God. You're really dead," she sobbed.

"But I'm still pretty, right?" I asked, trying again. She only cried harder. "Man, I am really out of practice at this comedy stuff. Maybe I should stick to knock-knock jokes."

Laura bawled in my arms for what felt like forever. Until my knees began to ache against the hardwood floor, and my toes fell asleep. When she finally pulled away from me and sat upright, her eyes were nearly swollen shut.

"Okay." She sniffled and fingered what was left of her mascara. "I can do this. Let's talk. We need a plan."

"A plan?" I groaned as I rocked back on my haunches and stood. "I just drank cow blood, and I have to be in bed in"—I checked the clock on the microwave—"four hours. Give or take."

"How can you sleep at a time like this?" Laura balked.

"Easy. I don't have any control over it." I scratched my chest where the tank top tag was digging into my skin.

Mandy nodded in agreement from the breakfast bar where she sat with a massive sandwich overflowing out of her hand. "Summer hours are a bitch for vamps," she said around a mouthful of food. "They barely get nine hours of sundown this time of year."

Laura blinked at me. "What about your appointment with Dr. Townsend Monday? What about Alicia and Serena's visit tomorrow? What about Will's funeral?" she added in an even more horrified voice. "You can't just lock yourself away every day and expect people not to ask questions, Jenna."

Mandy's nod of agreement was grimmer this time. "And if someone asks the wrong person those questions, you're going to have hella more problems to worry about than any shrink can help you with."

I looked from Mandy to Laura and threw up my hands. "What do you want me to say? I don't have a fucking clue where to even begin. Am I supposed to pack up and take off without saying a word to anyone? Just to stay off some super-secret vampire society's radar? What about the missing girls?" I turned back to Mandy. "How do you expect me to help you find them if the only time I can even function is the few hours in the middle of the night?"

"Hey." She held her free hand up in surrender. "I'm just pointing out facts here. Besides, the Scarlett Inn only operates at night. The brothel is run by vampires, remember?"

"A vampire brothel?" Laura's mouth dropped open. "These girls you're looking for are trapped in a *vampire* brothel? Aren't regular brothels bad enough?"

"What is *this*?" Mandy held up Agent Knight's business card. My jacket was draped over the barstool she sat on, and she had taken the liberty of searching its pockets while she stuffed her face.

"Nosy much?" I reached for the card, but she pulled her hand back.

"I told you not to involve the humans."

"You said no human doctors—"

"House Lilith doesn't just have spies in the hospitals," Mandy said, finally relenting and turning over the card before she lost her grip on her sandwich. "They're everywhere—in law enforcement, big business, you name it."

"How do they get around the daylight issue?" Laura asked. She was asking smarter questions than I had after I'd first found out about my new condition. But, to be fair, she hadn't just died or lost her partner. Temporary ignorance was a normal part of my grief cycle, apparently.

"The spies are either werewolves or humans," Mandy said. "*Special* humans," she added when I narrowed my eyes at her. "Most of them are half-sired, or in some sort of feeding arrangement with a vamp. They've been initiated and are registered, so they're safe."

"Half-sired? Feeding arrangement? Registered?" Laura put her face in her hands and shook her head. "I'm having trouble keeping up with all of this."

"Feel free to forget it." Mandy snorted. "Or at least don't repeat it to anyone. If you don't end up in a mental hospital first, House Lilith will put a price on your head. They don't mess around when it comes to protecting their own."

"Where does that leave Jenna?" Laura asked next.

Mandy licked what remained of her sandwich from her fingers and frowned at us. "That's the million-dollar question, isn't it?"

Chapter Eleven

It felt good to share my death with my sister. Though it had been so long since I'd been able to share my life with her, I had to wonder if I'd caved and told her my *deadly* secret out of sheer desperation. I hated that the knowledge could put her in danger, but just being associated with me was dangerous. At least now, the decision was hers to make. And she was still here. It mended something in my heart that I'd been sure would never be right again.

We stayed up talking until just before dawn, discussing the last decade of our separate lives since the next ten years seemed so uncertain. For both of us. Mandy left us to it, staking claim to my bed in my and Laura's old room—right after warning Laura that she'd dropkick Duncan if any leg-humping occurred. She was going to be a handful now that she had free rein of the house in her human form.

Laura followed me to my bedroom—to our mother's previous room. I could tell the nostalgia was a little overwhelming for her. I hadn't changed much in here either. The green plaid bedspread and matching curtains were as old as we were—though I had changed out the mini-blinds for light-blocking ones back when I worked on night patrol—and the fire hydrant lamp on the bedside table had been a gift we'd purchased together for Mom's thirtieth birthday. We'd been thirteen years old at the time. I'd had a paper route, and Laura had babysat the next-door neighbor's obnoxious kids for a few hours every day after school.

Laura lay down on the bed beside me, and we whispered in the dark, just like we had when we were in high school. I didn't want to upset her with stories about my job, so I let her do most of the talking. She filled me in on all the underground Hollywood gossip, and all the new trends and fad diets everyone was trying.

Right before the sun broke the sky, I felt the tingle of death coil up my spine and fill my skull. I had just enough time to warn Laura.

"Does it hurt?" she whispered, her hands wringing the end of her red ponytail under her chin. I tried to shake my head, but my body wasn't cooperating any longer. The breath froze in my lungs, and my eyes closed on Laura's anxious expression.

Fifteen hours later, my eyes opened to that same face. I blinked a few times, wondering if my vision was playing tricks on me again. Laura's red locks were now platinum blond.

"Finally!" She gasped, excitement chasing away her worry. "I've had all day to think about it, and I've figured it out!" She clapped her hands together and bounced on the edge of my bed.

"Have you been drinking coffee all day, too?" I rubbed a

hand over my face and down my neck to my chest to claw at the tag of my tank top. If I accomplished nothing else tonight, I decided I would at least shower and put on a fresh change of clothes. The mundane thought was quickly replaced by despair. "Alicia and Serena?"

Laura twirled a lock of her newly dyed hair. "I kept the visit short, but I think it was a pretty decent warm-up."

"Warm-up?" I asked, sitting and pulling myself to the edge of the bed. The achy, stiff feeling that had plagued me since waking at the morgue had let up after the cow blood, but it was slowly coming back.

"I mean, I was no Anastasia van de Velde," Laura said. She inspected her fingernails with a satisfied grin. "But Detective Laura Skye is a cakewalk in comparison."

I took a closer look at her and realized she was wearing one of my tee shirts and a pair of my cut-off shorts. "Please tell me you didn't…"

"Oh, I totally did." She gave me a devilish grin. "I've still got it, baby. David Steckleman can eat his heart out."

"Laura! This isn't some movie set. This is my fucking life!"

"What choice did I have?" She blinked at me. "Face it. You need my help."

"That wasn't right. You *know* that wasn't right."

"How well do you think it would have gone over if I'd

asked them to come back around eight-thirty?" She popped a fist on her hip. "Sorry, Jenna's dead to the world right now. Literally. But she'll be waking up later tonight to venture into gang territory for a pint of cow blood. Would you like to leave a message?" I made a pained face at the accusation, and she lifted both eyebrows before nodding at me. "Yeah. Teenybopper wolf girl spilled the beans."

"Dead girls gotta eat, too. What choice did I have?" I repeated her excuse with an apologetic shrug. "Speaking of, I'm starving."

"Oh, hell no." Laura held up a hand in my face. "You are not going back across the river. I don't care how indestructible you think you are. We'll buy some steak and put it in a blender."

I opened my mouth to protest but stopped when I realized I didn't actually know if that would work or not. Laura took it as a sign that I agreed with her idea and poked a finger on the side of my head.

"See! If you'd just think these things through, you wouldn't get yourself in so much trouble," she said. I gave her a wide-eyed glare and stood to fetch some clean clothes.

"So Alicia and Serena really thought you were me?" I shouted from my closet. Between Mandy and now Laura, it was in total disarray.

"Yes." Laura blew out a long sigh. "It was hard, though.

They were both crying, I mean, inconsolably sobbing. So I ended up crying, and then we were all blubbering."

I clutched a blouse to my chest and swallowed the lump building in the back of my throat. "Thanks." *It should have been me.* Not just bearing the weight of Will's family's grief, but lying dead—truly dead—in a cold locker at the morgue. If I weren't dead already, I would have died from the guilt and shame of my mistake.

"No problem," Laura answered from the doorway of my closet. I hadn't heard her sneak up, lost in my miserable thoughts. "I have your appointment with Dr. Townsend covered for tomorrow. And I'm pretty sure I convinced that beefcake FBI agent that you're a dead-end, too."

I spun around. "He called again?"

"He stopped by." Laura smirked and folded her arms. "If he weren't investigating you for Will's death, I would have invited him in to frisk me."

"Am I a suspect now? Did he say that?" Red pulsed at the edges of my vision, and I felt a cold trickle of panic creep up my spine.

"Not in so many words," Laura said. "But the way he acted—total asshat. He's clearly suspicious of you. I was cool as a cucumber, though. He really has no reason to question you further."

"We'll see." I waited for her to move out of the doorway

and circled around into the bathroom.

"So, we have grocery shopping to do tonight. Oh, and you have a sketch to draw for the captain," she added with a grimace. "I don't think one of my stick figure portraits would be very convincing. Luckily, that task doesn't require daylight."

"Yeah, that's going to be problematic since we don't want to alert the vampire mob family, or whoever the hell these big bad vamps are that Mandy is so afraid of. I guess I could fabricate a suspect, but I hate having to lie to the captain." I tugged at the rubber band in my hair and winced when it ripped out several strands with its departure.

Laura clicked her tongue at me and then hovered over my shoulder, inspecting herself in the bathroom mirror as she mimicked my sour expression. Our reflections hadn't been this identical since graduation. Of course, her eyebrows were better pruned than mine, and she had fewer split ends.

"I told you that rubber band was a bad idea," she said in my ear as she picked a stray hair off my shoulder. "I'll do a hot oil treatment on your hair while you're sleeping tomorrow."

I crinkled my nose at her. "You're going to play with me like a freaking doll while I'm out?"

"I wish someone would primp me while I slept. Think of all the time that would save?" Her eyes lit up with hopeful cheer. "Maybe I ought to suggest that to the spa I frequent."

A squeal ripped through the house, and then Mandy was in the doorway of the bathroom, her hands on her hips and murder on her face. "That *rodent* of yours crapped on the kitchen floor, and I *stepped* in it." She lifted up her foot to show us the smudge of green between her toes.

I couldn't contain my grin. "Don't worry. Zee new maid will take care of it."

"Grrrr." Her lips curled back, and I half expected her to bark at me. "I'm done sitting around here waiting for you to get your shit together. I'm going to look for the Scarlett Inn tonight, with or without you."

I nodded and held up the clean shirt. "I just need a shower first."

"And food," Laura added, pointing her finger at me and then Mandy. "I'm going to call a cab and make a quick dash to the grocery store."

"You can take the Bronco if you want," I offered.

Laura made a horrified face. "I'll pass. I haven't driven a *real* car in years, let alone that tin can."

"Could you clean up the dog shit first?" Mandy pinched her nose. "If I go back in that kitchen, I'm going to yack."

"Oh, grief. You big baby." Laura groaned and pushed past her and out of the bathroom.

Mandy took her place beside me and propped her foot up

on the edge of the sink before ripping several tissues from a box on the counter. She grumbled under her breath as she wiped her toes clean, and then grabbed my hairbrush and began grooming herself.

"A little privacy?" I blinked at her and held up the shirt again.

Mandy grunted and swiped my curling iron before exiting the bathroom. I closed the door behind her and hung my blouse on the hook behind it. And then it occurred to me that I'd forgotten the rest of my outfit. I'd been too distracted by Laura's makeover and what it meant—what it *could* mean. It was still weighing on my mind, ping-ponging between guilt and hope. A queasy feeling stirred deep in my gut, and I couldn't decide if it was more from the jumble of conflicting emotions, or the cow blood disagreeing with me.

I ducked out of the bathroom long enough to grab some underwear and a pair of jeans and then jumped into the shower, cranking the water up as hot as I could stand. There was a chill in my bones that I couldn't seem to shake. It had improved after my first postmortem meal, but it was coming back, along with the stiffness. Was this normal for a vampire? Did it only improve with blood? I hated that I had so many questions and not nearly enough answers.

As I breathed in the steam from the shower, my thoughts returned to Laura and her doppelganger act. I had to admit, it was pretty brilliant. And Laura seemed rejuvenated by the new role, even if it didn't pay as much as playing Judge Henry's saucy court reporter. I guess we all like to feel needed. But how long would it last? How long before someone figured out that we'd pulled the ol' switcheroo? How long before Laura tired of my boring, Midwestern lifestyle and yearned for the glamour and fame she'd left behind? I was betting one Missouri winter would be all it took.

Allowing myself to look at this as if it were a permanent solution would be foolish, but hope bubbled up anyway. Maybe a better plan would emerge in time, but for now, I could appreciate Laura's efforts and make the most of an otherwise sucky situation.

The doorbell rang as I turned off the shower, and I wrapped myself in a towel before Mandy barged in.

"That ugly green car that stopped by last night is back," she announced. "And some shmuck is on the front porch with flowers."

Vin. *Ugh.* He just didn't know when to quit. "Maybe he'll go away?" I suggested. The doorbell rang twice more, and I felt the corners of my mouth instinctively sag down my face. "Shit."

"The FBI guy drove an SUV," Mandy said, folding her arms and narrowing her eyes at me. "Who's this joker?"

"The morgue doctor."

She made a face. "Creepy."

"You have no idea." I groaned and shooed her out of the bathroom. "Let me throw on my clothes real quick, and I'll take care of it."

I towel-dried my hair and dressed in a rush while Vin abused the doorbell some more. By the time I finally answered, I was ready to strangle him.

"*What?*" I said, biting the word off like an expletive as I ripped the door open. To Vin's credit, he didn't fall backward down the front steps this time.

"I want a do-over." He lifted his chin and thrust a new bouquet of blood-red roses at me. He was in a pair of charcoal slacks and a green dress shirt tonight, and the glasses were gone. "You caught me off-guard last night, but I came prepared this time."

"Prepared?" I ignored the outstretched flowers and ran a hand through my wet hair. "Vin, you're being ridiculous."

"Really? Am I?" He lifted an eyebrow and then pulled a bag of blood out of his pants pocket.

A gasp escaped me before I could contain the euphoric sensation that shot through my core. I blinked, and the world turned red. Vin gave me a satisfied grin, but it disappeared when I grabbed the front of his shirt and jerked him inside, shoving the door closed behind us.

The living room was dark, the only light coming from the

porch light slipping through the curtains over the front window. The red lens of my hunger didn't seem to care one way or another. I could see the outlines of the furniture and the walls clear as day. I could see Vin, blindly groping for something to anchor himself in the sea of darkness.

I snatched the flowers and the blood from him, crushing them against my chest. The roses felt off. Rubbery. "These are fake," I hissed, forcing the conversation in the first random direction I could come up with, anything to steer it away from the fact that I'd responded so viscerally to the bag of blood.

"They'll never die," he whispered, his eyes following the sound of my voice. "Just like you."

"Are you calling me fake?"

"I think you know exactly what I'm calling you." Vin's voice slithered dangerously through the dark, and I could feel all the things hidden in his words. The dare. The threat. The invitation. "You didn't have a pulse, Jenna. I haven't seen you in daylight since you woke up on my table Friday night. Just after sunset, if I remember correctly."

My body reacted without warning. I dropped the flowers and the blood, and then I was pressed against Vin, pinning his back to the wall. He grunted, but I couldn't tell if it was in pain or surprise. Maybe both.

"What do you want from me?" The words felt raw in my

throat. I was caught somewhere between begging and maiming. The galloping pulse in his throat was inches away, and my eyes locked onto it as the tips of my canines grazed my bottom lip. My breath rushed in and out, moving the little hairs trailing around the side of Vin's neck, and he shuddered.

"What do you want from *me*?" he asked.

I licked my lips and swallowed, trying to talk myself out of what I *really* wanted, and pulled Vin away from the wall. I bent over and collected the fake roses, slapping them against Vin's chest as I stood. He made a dejected noise as if he'd actually wanted me to bite him. The weirdo. I yanked the front door open and unceremoniously shoved him out onto the porch.

"Wait! Jenna—" He stumbled backward and caught himself on the railing alongside the steps before springing right back up. I slammed the door in his face so hard that the picture of my mother and Maggie fell off the wall, the glass shattering as it hit the floor.

I stood perfectly still, my hands balled into fists against my chest, and held my breath until I thought I might pass out. Which felt like forever. *Did vampires need to breathe?* Just one more answerless question falling like invisible confetti around my head.

When the kitchen light clicked on, I jumped in surprise. Mandy's long shadow dissected the living room. She stood with her hands on her hips, modeling a pair of my cropped yoga pants and a workout tank top.

"What is *that?*" She made a disgusted face and pointed at the abandoned blood bag on the floor. I'd conveniently forgotten to throw it out with Vin and the fake flowers.

"Dinner," I answered, picking it up and inspecting the label. O negative. Vin had gone all out.

Mandy's mouth dropped open, and she sucked in a slow gasp. "He knows?" she whisper-screamed at me. "Of course, he knows! Maybe you should just hang a fucking neon sign in the window."

"I didn't tell him," I whisper-screamed back at her, worried that Vin might still be loitering on the porch. "He guessed, okay? This is *so* not my fault."

"You suck at being a bloodsucker." Mandy scowled at me as I sniffed the blood bag, and then she turned on her heel and stormed into the kitchen. "I'm going to eat something before we leave."

The doorbell rang again. I ground my teeth together and decided that if Vin couldn't take a hint, maybe I *would* take a bite out of him. Either that or uninstall the doorbell. I threw the door open with an unrestrained snarl.

"Oh!" Laura jumped and dropped a paper grocery sack. She'd made it up the driveway and onto the porch with three of them squeezed in a bear hug. "Shit," she grumbled. "I hope that one didn't have the eggs in it."

"Sorry." I scooped up the rogue bag and inspected its contents as Laura wobbled past me. "I thought you were someone else."

Her cheeks flushed, and her brows drew together. "I saw Vin as he was leaving. What did he want?"

"To make me crazy," I said, only half-joking. "Can you believe that he's still trying to convince me that we slept together the night of senior prom? The jerk didn't even have the balls to ask me to go. I turned down Max Collins waiting for Vin to ask, and he never did."

"Didn't Max Collins turn out to be gay?" Laura said over her shoulder as we headed into the kitchen and past Mandy, who was sitting at the dining table with a sandwich and a bag of chips.

"So? Collins was hot—still is—and he could dance," I said. "It would have been the best night ever. Instead, I was stuck at home, sobbing into a bowl of popcorn while watching *All Dogs Go to Heaven* with Mom." I dumped the grocery sack on the kitchen counter a little too forcefully, and Laura made a pained face. "There weren't any eggs in there," I said defensively. When her face didn't change, I checked the bag again just to be sure.

"Um, Vin *did* actually ask you to go to prom," Laura said, setting her bags down beside mine and wringing her hands together.

"What? No, he didn't. I would have remembered *that*." I hated to admit it, but once upon a time, I'd actually had a crush on the jerk.

Laura tossed a lock of her newly blond hair over her shoulder and cleared her throat. "Since we're mending bridges and cleaning out closets and all, I suppose there's something I should tell you."

My stomach fluttered, and my fingers dug into the bag of blood that was clutched in my hand. "Laura?" I said in a warning voice. "Please tell me you didn't."

She cleared her throat again as if she had been preparing this monologue for some time. Like, possibly for ten years. Her eyes struggled to meet mine, but when they did, she made her confession. "I slept with Vin the night of prom."

Chapter Twelve

I was going to be sick. I was sure of it. "You did what?"

"Oh, snap." Mandy paused her face-stuffing and pushed back from the table to get a better view of us, almost as if she anticipated a cat fight. I hadn't crossed the possibility off my list yet.

"I'm so sorry." Tears welled in Laura's eyes, but she had the good sense to back away from me and circled the breakfast bar, putting a barrier between us. "Jason Tanner had just dumped me, and he'd convinced the entire football team that I had chlamydia. No one—*no one*—had asked me to senior prom." Laura sniffled, and her face contorted with shame. "I was on the ballot for prom queen one week, and then the joke of the school the next. I was the captain of the cheerleading squad and voted most likely to become a star, and then I was a dateless laughingstock."

"But you *did* become a star," I said, struggling to keep my sympathy in check. Laura crying was like kryptonite, and she knew it. But it wasn't enough to excuse what she'd done this time. "A few bad weeks doesn't justify sleeping with your sister's crush. That's low. That's lower than low."

"I know," she said, resentment shadowing her words. "I was just so…so jealous. I was the most popular girl in school, and yet, somehow, I couldn't land a single suitor for prom.

But my nerdy sister had two?"

"So you thought you'd help yourself? You entitled cow!" I slapped the blood bag on the counter before I ruptured it and gripped the lip of the sink with both hands. "Why Vin? Why not go with Collins?"

Laura shrugged. "Max had already asked you. When Vin asked me, assuming I *was* you, I figured that was my only chance."

"But you didn't even go to prom. So what was the point?"

"I chickened out," Laura said, covering her face with her hands. "When you didn't cave and accept Max's offer, I felt like such an asshole."

I snorted. "Sounds like the shoe fit."

"Yeah." She sighed and looked up at me again. "I felt too guilty to go through with it, and I knew if I did—if I pretended to be you—someone would eventually figure it out. Then I'd be an even bigger joke than I already was. I'd be remembered as pathetic Laura Skye, the girl who was so desperate that she impersonated her nerdy sister so she could steal her even nerdier prom date."

I pointed a finger at her over the counter. "If this is an apology, I recommend that you stop calling me a nerd. I might not have been a cheerleader, but let me remind you that we're identical twins. I was every bit as hot as you were. Bitch."

"Sorry." Laura blushed again and folded her arms. "I didn't mean it like that. You were just…smart. Smarter than me anyway."

I rolled my eyes. "Like that's an accomplishment."

Laura's jaw clenched, and she lifted her chin, but she didn't return the insult. "I deserved that."

"Yup," I agreed, nowhere near finished with her.

"I guess this makes us even." She held out a hand, palm up. "I mean, you went and got yourself killed. I just slept with some guy you had a crush on."

"Not even close. I didn't die on purpose!"

"It wasn't like he was your boyfriend. You never even went on a date with him." She couldn't be serious. Could she?

Our eyes locked in a staring match, but before Laura had the chance to yield and look away first, Mandy huffed out an amused laugh and bit off a chunk of her sandwich.

"If I had a sister and she banged my crush, I'd eat her," she said. "I'd eat him, too." Laura and I both gaped at her. "What?" Mandy said. "I'm just saying. In wolf form, obviously," she added as an afterthought.

"Oh, well, in that case…" I curled up my nose at her and grabbed the blood bag off the counter. It was hard not to feel like a hypocrite as I turned it over in my hand, trying to figure out the best way to proceed. A kitchen knife would be messy, but I could never seem to find the scissors when I needed them. I pinched at the stopper in the neck of the bag and attempted to unscrew it.

"Where did that come from?" Laura asked as if she'd only

just noticed it.

"Your lover boy. *Tramp.*"

Laura groaned and folded her arms. I was expecting some more groveling, but before she made it that far, her pitiful face blanched. "He knows? Why does *he* know? I thought you couldn't stand him?"

"I can't! Thanks to *you.*" I gave her a dirty look, the first of many I was sure I'd be subjecting her to over the next few days. Or weeks. "He couldn't figure out that he was screwing my twin and not me but, somehow, he guessed that I'm a vampire. Figures."

I gave up on decorum and chomped down on the corner of the bag. My canines extended instinctively and punctured the thin plastic. Cold blood gushed into my mouth. Cold *human* blood. It was considerably better than cow. A shiver rattled my shoulders, and I moaned, shamelessly forgetting that I was standing in my kitchen in front of my sister and Mandy.

"That is so gross," Laura whined, covering her eyes with one hand.

Mandy grunted her agreement, apparently forgetting that she'd eaten a whole freaking vampire just a couple of nights ago. So what if she'd been in wolf form? Did that really make it any more kosher? Even Duncan, curled up under Mandy's chair and licking crumbs off the floor, lifted his head to make a distasteful noise at me.

I slurped at the bag, draining it within seconds, and then held it upside down, encouraging the last few drops into my mouth like Laura and I used to do with ice pops when we were kids. I debated cutting it open and licking the sticky remnants off the inside, but from Mandy's alarmed expression, I guessed I'd already gotten weird enough.

I crumpled the empty bag and waited for Laura to uncover her eyes. "Any other deep, dark secrets you'd like to divulge now that I'm well fed and less likely to bite you?"

Her eyes widened. "You wouldn't," she said, looking unsure enough about the answer that I took offense.

"Depends," I snapped. "Who else has said my name while you were boning them?"

"No one." Laura pressed a palm to her chest. "I swear. I'll even tell Vin myself if that's what you want. We're still young. You could have another chance with him—"

"Ugh!" I threw the empty blood bag at her and huffed. "I don't want your sloppy seconds. Or your *chlamydia*. Besides, I just spent the last ten years hating him. That's not something I can just shut off like that." I snapped my fingers in her face.

Laura's eyes watered again, and she swallowed and looked away from me. "I didn't think so."

"Oh, please. You know I wasn't talking about us." I sighed out a frustrated breath and rubbed a hand over my face.

I couldn't deal with her crying right now. And I couldn't

stomach this rage without lashing out at her. I needed to get out of the house for a while, and maybe find some way to dispel the anxiety tying my insides into knots. The fresh blood had helped—I felt limber and warm, almost like a real person again.

"It's pushing eleven," Mandy said, standing up from the table and wiping her hands down the front of my yoga pants. "I'm ready to find my girls. Are you coming with me or not?" She glanced away from me long enough to growl at Duncan when he licked a crumb off her foot.

"We can take the Bronco back to the crime scene." I shot Laura a wary glance. Her eyebrows knitted together as she looked up at me.

"I charged your backup phone. Please take it with you," she said.

I nodded, already forgiving her despite my better judgment.

We were sisters, after all.

Mandy looked cute in Maggie's old off-duty vest with its little, buttoned pockets and fur lining. Of course, I'd never tell her that. And certainly not while she was in wolf form and staring at me from the passenger seat like she wanted to eat my face off. At least I wouldn't have to listen to her mouth off for a while, which allowed me plenty of time to think about Laura's bombshell and to wallow in the new wave of guilt that came with it.

I'd been a total bitch to Vin. No, I'd been something that began with a capital C. I mean, it wasn't exactly my fault, but still. I felt bad. I needed to apologize and explain things at the very least. Did that mean I was up for his courting antics? *Eh.* The jury was still out.

Vin was a nice enough guy, but like I'd told Laura—I couldn't go from hating him for ten years to being wooed overnight. My high school crush had fizzled out a long time ago. Maybe too long ago to be rekindled. There was also the small matter of me being one of the undead now. And the awkward fact that I hadn't been good at dating when I was alive. How was I supposed to manage it as a bloodsucker with such a tight daylight curfew?

Vin knowing my secret was just one straw on the camel's back. I was torn about how I should feel about it. On the one hand, it was one more person in danger because of me. One more name on a list growing much too long, much too fast. On the other hand, I wouldn't have to lie to him to get around all my new vices and limitations. And I had really, *really* enjoyed the blood bag he'd brought me. I certainly wouldn't mind that becoming a regular thing. But was that enough reason to date him? It seemed...wrong. Even worse than dating him out of guilt for the way I'd treated him all these years.

Ever since I'd died, life had become so damned complicated. I felt like I was just hanging on for the ride, and the destination was anyone's guess.

The traffic thinned out long before the Bronco reached the industrial park with the warehouse Will and I had staked out. A single security light illuminated the uneven pavement. Weeds and tree saplings pushed up through the cracks and clung to the rusty sheet metal and crumbling cinder blocks fashioned into warehouses that hadn't been used—at least not for anything legal—for decades, and yellow police tape marked off the door leading down to the basement where everything had gone so horribly wrong.

The moon was a slice shy of full. It added a blue tint to the scene, claiming dominance over the pale security light. I parked the Bronco between the same two buildings Will and I had used for cover and killed the engine. It was too late to think better of it.

Wait, Skye. Will's voice surfaced in my mind. *We don't know how many are down there. Get back in the car, and we'll call for backup.*

What if they're too late? What if there are girls down there? We have to do something.

I'd let panic get the best of me. And glory, and pride, and wrath. Hell, I'd covered half of the seven deadly sins without a second thought.

The Bronco shook, and a sharp, grating noise broke the silence. My gaze snapped to Mandy. She whined and licked her muzzle before pulling her paw away from her open door, the edge of which was now jammed against one of the buildings the Bronco was sandwiched between. If I hadn't known she was a person under all that fur, I would have been surprised that she'd managed to open the door without assistance. And even more surprised that she hadn't just jumped through the open window.

I sighed and scrunched my lips to one side. "Subtle."

She growled at me and then hopped out of the truck. I grabbed the Browning out of the glovebox and tucked it into the waistband of my jeans before joining her. I had my Glock in a bra holster under my right arm. I wasn't sure either of them would do me any good if we encountered another vampire, considering how well that had gone the last time, but there were werewolves and these *special* humans Mandy had mentioned. I was betting I'd stand a better chance against them.

Mandy sniffed the ground along the foundation of the warehouse, cuing up my fuzzy memory again. I realized I'd made it to the basement door first as my fingers closed around the gritty handle. The yellow police tape crinkled as Mandy nudged me aside and slipped under it.

Wait for me, rookie. I go in first.

I touched my shoulder, remembering the feel of Will's

hand as he pulled me away from the stairwell and moved ahead of me, disappearing into the dark. The smell of wet mold was suffocating. A steady drip echoed from somewhere nearby, and the temperature was at least twenty degrees cooler than the sweltering night air outside.

How could anyone think this was a good place to sex it up? Even with underage werewolf girls? The thought bothered me. *Think*, I commanded my brain. But before I arrived at the all too obvious answer, a thump sounded from overhead. Mandy's yellow eyes met mine, and she panted, anticipation sending the hairs along her back up.

Of course. The Scarlett Inn was upstairs. Not down here in this creepy empty basement. The vampire had been a decoy. And I'd fallen for it and gotten myself and Will killed in the process.

I lifted my hoodie and drew the Glock before motioning for Mandy to follow me to the opposite set of stairs tucked in the back corner. She darted ahead, her paws soundless on the dusty, concrete floor.

There was police tape marking this entrance off, too. I knew the PD had probably scoured the whole building, but they hadn't had a werewolf who knew what scents were worth tracking. And they probably hadn't encountered any suspects while they went about their business in the daylight.

My heart pumped violently in my chest, my pulse beating out a steady rhythm that was almost human. I wondered if the

O negative had something to do with that, or if it was just the adrenaline building in my veins. My vision turned red again, and the color transferred to my memories, staining Will's vacant expression as he lay dead on the basement floor.

Mandy waited at the foot of the stairs, but I hesitated, frozen in time. Ghost shots echoed through my mind. So many of them that I had to wonder if a box of fireworks had been set off. Then I heard Will's gun click empty.

Get out of here, Skye! Run!

Will had known something wasn't right. But I couldn't just leave him down here. I inched through the dark, moving around the dented remains of a rusty furnace unit, my sweaty fingers clenched around my gun. Moonlight filtered through a small, dirty window high on the wall. It cut a ribbon of visibility across the basement, painting a rectangle of light on the dusty floor.

That's where I found Will, his whole body lifted up into the air, shaking as if he were being electrocuted. The vampire—Raphael, my sire—held my partner's back against his chest. His face was hidden in shadow, pressed into the side of Will's neck. But I could see Will's face. The terror and despair in his swollen eyes. The glowing white of his teeth as his scream died. As he died. As I let him die.

I couldn't move, at least not beyond the panicked tremble that shook my body in time with Will's. The sound—the gnashing and sucking of skin and sinew—did something to my psyche. I was petrified, glued to the spot by disbelief and confusion. If I couldn't trust my own eyes, what else was there to do?

Die. That's what I can do, *I thought as the creature cast Will's lifeless body to the floor. I blinked, and then he was on me. I hadn't even seen him move. The surprise of Raphael's attack triggered my training, and my finger began to work again, squeezing off a series of rounds that did about as much as Will's had. Which was nothing. A few seconds later, I was dead, too.*

Mandy made an impatient snort from the base of the stairs and tapped a paw on the bottom step. I shook my head to clear it, pushing the grief and shame out of my mind for the time being. I knew what I was up against now. I wouldn't fail again. *I can't fail again*, I thought, sticking close to Mandy as we ascended the stairs.

Werewolf or not, she was just a girl. And she was counting on me. Along with a few dozen more just like her.

Chapter Thirteen

The warehouse hadn't looked any different than the rest of the abandoned buildings in the industrial park. At least not from the outside. And Mathis hadn't mentioned what else they'd discovered at the scene. I knew it was his job to keep the details of the case confidential, but I was still annoyed with him for withholding so much.

On the second floor of the warehouse, the ceiling was scorched with a blackened circle, mirroring one on the floor directly beneath it. There had been a fire here recently, though it looked as if it had burned out prematurely. Not much had been left behind to feed it. Mandy snorted and nodded her muzzle at me as if she wanted to say something. I made a mental note to ask her about it later and ventured farther into the room.

Dark red curtains hung from the ceiling, covering a good chunk of the cracked drywall and boarded-up windows. Several disassembled bedframes were stacked against the far wall, and a soiled mattress lay abandoned in the middle of the floor. It summoned a low growl from Mandy when she sniffed it. She nodded her muzzle again as if to suggest she'd gotten what she needed, and then took off across the room, heading for an exit in the back corner.

This new set of stairs only went down one flight, to the

empty ground floor that looked as if it might have been a factory floor or receiving center at one time. A maze of conveyor tables zigzagged through the room, and piles of rotting cardboard boxes created an obstacle course that would have been hazardous to navigate even in daylight. I barely managed with the aid of my blood vision, my gun relinquished to one hand so I could climb over a metal desk angled in my path. My hip cracked into the corner of it as I dismounted, and a nest of rats hissed and squeaked as they fled from a box beneath the desk.

I swallowed a squeak of my own and hurried after Mandy. She dipped her nose to the ground and increased her pace, rushing toward an exterior door at the back of the building. Hinges groaned, and metal scraped the concrete floor. Then I was running to catch up.

Mandy had locked onto a scent, and she didn't seem to care that I was on this hunt with her. She slipped through the crack in the door and out of sight, sending a stab of panic through my chest. I rushed into the alley after her, my gun grasped in both hands again. My eyes darted in all directions. Then I caught sight of the green dog vest as she disappeared around the corner of the next building up.

I swore under my breath and chased after her. She moved so fast—which meant that our suspect was swift, too. And likely another werewolf. *Great.* Just what I needed.

Before I'd made it to the alley Mandy had turned down, a howl filled the air. The sound echoed all around me and sent a tremor through my bones, but it didn't slow me down. I pushed onward, my breath scorching my lungs and my legs aching for reprieve.

Where was my superhuman strength? The thought grated on me. Raphael had been fast and incredibly strong. Why didn't I have that? Was I not only a flawed detective but also a defective vampire? So far, my new existence appeared to come with far more cons than pros, and I still didn't know whom I was supposed to lodge my complaints with.

At the mouth of the next alley, I paused to catch my breath and evaluate the scene. With the red vision, my surroundings glowed with stark white outlines. Movement caught my attention just as a wolf landed on top of a rusty dumpster up ahead. Mandy yipped and shook her muzzle.

Her doggy tantrum was short-lived, and then she leapt at her mark—a stocky man in a ragged vest and blue jeans. He had a long tangle of dark hair and a matching mustache. Mandy looked as if she were trying to bite it right off his face as he clung to the broken end of a ladder attached to the building. I guessed he'd used the dumpster as a launch pad. The ladder was at least ten feet off the ground.

The man swatted at Mandy with one arm and bared his teeth as he tried to walk his legs up the side of the building.

An unnatural growl stirred in his throat. Mandy returned it full force before propping her front paws up on the wall and closing her jaws around his ankle. He kicked her in the face with his free foot. The heel of his boot bit into her muzzle, drawing a wounded yip from her.

"Down!" I shouted, taking aim with my gun. The man turned his yellow eyes on me at the same time Mandy did, as if he assumed I'd made the request of him. But as soon as Mandy dropped all four paws back to the dumpster's lid, I put a bullet through the man's forearm.

He screamed and fell to the patch of gravel and weeds below. So, bullets worked on werewolves. *Score one for me!* That was a relief. I kept my gun trained on the guy and shook my head as Mandy hopped down from the dumpster and moved in on him.

"You can't eat him," I told her. "At least not until I ask my questions."

The man wrapped a hand around his injured arm and kicked at the gravel, pushing his back up against the building behind him. My breath tightened at the sight of blood oozing through his fingers. I wondered how much of a fight Mandy would put up if I tried to take a bite out of him first.

He sneered up at me, sending the edges of his greasy mustache curling over his upper lip. "The boss knows I'm here. He sent me himself," he said. "If I don't return, Scarlett can kiss her deal with the pack goodbye."

"What deal?" I bit my tongue too late, and the man's eyes lit with understanding. He gave me a throaty laugh and shook his head.

"So the royal bitch is on the run again." He spat at my feet.

"What deal?" I demanded. I wondered if he meant the same deal Mandy had mentioned before—a ride for a bite. Mandy growled and inched closer to him, but his expression grew bored.

"Don't matter now. Looks like she left our turf. You better, too, if you know what's good for you," he said, his eyes flickering yellow as he stared up at me. The bones in his jaw moved in ways no human's ever should, and I lifted my gun higher, angling it at his face rather than his chest.

"I wouldn't do that if I were you," I warned him.

Mandy's growl cut off suddenly. She lifted her head and turned to glance behind me with a whimper.

"Mandy? Io that you?" An amused voice asked.

I took my eyes off the man at my feet long enough to get a look at the newcomer. And the silver-barreled shotgun aimed at my head. Part of me wanted to believe that I didn't have anything to worry about, but I clearly wasn't on the same level as my sire had been. Would bullets hurt? Could they actually kill me? I honestly wasn't sure.

The man holding the shotgun was clean-shaven and wore a leather jacket. I wouldn't have guessed that he was with the mustachioed scumbag Mandy had tracked down, but apparently, werewolves were capable of just as many flavors as humans. Or vampires.

"Report back to Marcel," the newcomer ordered our bleeding catch. "I'll take care of these two."

"I don't think so," I said, my gun trained on the fallen man's face.

"What are you going to do, sweetheart?" Leather Jacket snorted. "Shoot him? Go ahead." The smirk on Mustache's face melted into a grimace.

"Just tell me where the Scarlett Inn is," I said through clenched teeth. "Then we can all go our separate ways." Thankfully, Mandy didn't protest my suggestion.

"The Scarlett Inn?" Leather Jacket scoffed. "What's a good girl like you want with the Scarlett Inn? Are you looking for a job, sweetheart?"

"Or maybe she has a thing for scrawny little wolf girls," Mustache said, casting a sideways glance at Mandy. She had migrated behind the dumpster, retreating from Leather Jacket's line of sight.

"This doesn't have to get ugly." I tried to relax my shoulders to match their confidence, but it just wasn't coming to me. I could smell Mustache's blood. The tangy scent stung the back of my throat. "Just tell me what I want to know."

Leather Jacket narrowed his eyes at me. "You think we'd be here if we knew the inn had moved? Who the hell are you anyway? One of Ursula's scouts? Or just a random vamp Scarlett screwed over?"

A rifle cocked, and another body joined us in the alley. This one I recognized. FBI Special Agent Roman Knight. In full black under the pale light of the moon, he was almost invisible, save for his white halo of hair.

"Having a party without me, boys?" he asked Leather Jacket. Then his eyes fell on me and hardened. "Lose the shotgun, Arnie."

"She one of yours, Knight? I've got splinter rounds loaded in this thing. It'd be a shame if one of them ended up in her heart."

"It would be," Agent Knight agreed in a flat voice. "But I can thread needles with this machine. You and your boy over there would both have a third eye before she hit the ground."

Leather Jacket gritted his teeth, but he lowered the shotgun and tossed it into a tangle of brush growing up through the chain-link fence that surrounded the industrial park. He placed his hands on his head and dropped to his knees. His eyes stayed locked on me, a teasing sharpness to them that suggested we weren't finished.

Agent Knight pulled a pair of handcuffs from his pocket

and slung his rifle over his shoulder and across his back as he approached. His casual resolve unnerved me. Did he know how much danger he was in? He didn't seem to.

"Wait," I said, lowering my gun to my side. "I was questioning them."

"So I heard." He gave me a patronizing glare. "Funny, I was sure your captain told me you were placed on leave." He pressed a button on a small device attached to his shoulder holster and spoke into it. "Suspect apprehended. Bring the car around." After he'd released the button, he looked up at me again. "You should probably go, unless you'd like to ride along down to the field office and explain why you're interfering with an FBI investigation."

I swallowed, trying to calm the frustrated rage that was eating me alive. "You don't understand. These men, they're not what you think. They're—" I glanced back at where Mustache had been sitting, but he was gone. Mandy, too. "Shit!" I spun in a wide circle, searching the alley and the brush and bramble along the fence.

"I hope that *dog* of yours is collared and licensed. Her type doesn't fare well in pounds," Agent Knight said, ignoring the fact that the other man was missing.

Leather Jacket—Arnie—snickered. "I'll make bail by tomorrow. Then you and I'll have us a good time, sweetheart." He gave me a shameless and lusty once-over.

Agent Knight shoved him toward the alley that opened onto the main road running through the industrial park.

"Don't hold your breath, *sweetheart*," he said. Then he shot a look over his shoulder at me. "Go home, and don't let me catch you at my crime scene again."

I stared after him as he hauled off my only lead. Wrath curdled in my gut, and my hands shook. I had an awful urge to break something. Like maybe his face.

Mandy's warning about involving humans came back to me, but there was nothing I could do about it. Not legally. A werewolf in FBI custody didn't seem like a good idea even if there hadn't been a secret vampire society to police supernaturals. I wondered what kind of attention this would end up attracting. And then I wondered how I was going to evade it.

A black SUV stopped at the end of the alley. I ducked behind the building and watched from the shadows as Agent Knight opened the back door and shoved the werewolf inside. Then he opened the front door and climbed into the passenger's seat. I caught a glimpse of a woman behind the wheel. She was dressed all in black, just like Agent Knight, with black hair knotted in a braid over her shoulder. She turned slowly as if sensing me, and bright green eyes met mine just before Agent Knight's door snapped shut, concealing them behind tinted windows.

"It's not that bad," Laura said. "Just a scratch really." She'd pulled her hair back into a messy bun and put on a pair of rimless reading glasses to get a better look at the damage.

Mandy sat curled up in a barstool at the kitchen counter, one leg tucked under her and the other upright so she could rest her chin on her knee. Laura dabbed a cotton swab covered with antibiotic ointment over a cut that ran along half the length of the girl's eyebrow. Then she carefully stretched two butterfly strips over the wound to hold it closed. She'd already cleaned and covered the road rash on Mandy's forearm and had her rinse the blood out of her mouth. Her lip was split and swollen on one side.

Mandy watched me as I paced the kitchen, but she didn't say anything as Laura finished patching her up. She'd reappeared in the alley in time to witness me taking my frustrated rage out on a dumpster. Our ride home had been tense, and I was worried that she knew how hard it was for me to sit next to her for half an hour with as much blood as she was leaking all over the place. In her wolf form, she seemed to have a keen awareness of those sorts of visceral emotions.

My hunger had evolved. After the blood bag, I'd felt like

a million bucks. Then, just a few short hours later, I'd been reduced to a ravenous train wreck. I didn't understand how it was possible. Had our useless investigation really taken that much out of me? Or had the small bit of human blood I'd had trigger some full-blown addiction?

I slurped at the thick cow blood Laura had blended up for me while we were gone and tried not to focus on the fact that it tasted like ass, especially now that I'd had the good stuff. My stomach grumbled a painful protest, and for a moment, I feared that I might have another Exorcist experience. Maybe Laura hadn't strained the mutilated cow bits as well as she'd thought.

"Better?" Mandy asked, eyeing me cautiously.

I nodded and swallowed the last of the blood with a wince. "Who were those guys?" I blurted, jumping right into the questions I'd wanted to ask since the warehouse.

Mandy sucked in a sharp breath, and her eyes unfocused as she glanced away from me. "Wolves from the Moreau Pack. I didn't recognize the one I tracked outside, but the other one is Arnold Moreau—the alpha's little brother."

"He told Mustache to report back to Marcel—"

Mandy flinched at the name. "That's him," she said, her voice barely a whisper.

Laura gathered up the bandage wrappers and sighed as she circled the kitchen counter to throw them into the wastebasket under the sink. "I don't like this at all. You're supposed to be on leave."

"You sound like that prick FBI agent." I pulled out a chair at the table and dropped onto it, discarding the sticky plastic tumbler next to a giant first aid kit that looked like a tackle box. It'd been around since we were toddlers. Laura had been a careful child—me, not so much.

Mandy's eyes found me again. "He smelled like vampire," she said grimly.

"No way." I shook my head. "He called me during the day."

"I didn't say he *was* a vampire," Mandy said. "He *smelled* like vampire. As in, he was with one recently. Whether he knows that or not is another story. Either way, he can't be trusted."

"Agreed." I folded my arms. "What about upstairs—what were you trying to tell me then?"

She blinked a few times as if catching up with the present. The mention of Marcel Moreau had shaken her, and I didn't have the heart to ask what I was pretty sure I already knew the answer to.

"The fire," she finally said. "I put it out. The night before you and your partner met Raphael."

"Why? Who started it?"

"One of Scarlett's minions, I'm sure. That it's still

standing is probably why Raphael made an appearance." Mandy pulled her other leg up and hugged them both to her chest. Her jaw clenched, and I could tell she was trying to steel herself against what she was about to share. "That's what they do when the Inn's been compromised. They move the girls out and burn the place down to destroy any lingering scent trails. One of the older girls told me before she died—before she was *murdered*—that when a place goes up in flames, it means they'll be moving to a new city soon."

"Where would they keep the girls in the meantime?" I asked.

Mandy shook her head. "They have money. They could bribe a client with a big enough place, or buy a property if they wanted to. They could be anywhere."

I remembered from Will's investigation notes that the warehouse belonged to an out-of-state trust. We'd had a hell of a time tracking down the names of the trustees, and the few that we did reach by phone didn't seem to know much at all about the property—though they all agreed that we would have to get a search warrant if we wanted inside. With nothing more than a tip from a petty crook, no judge would sign off on that. And that's how Will and I had ended up staking out the place for my first week on vice.

"A fire seems awfully risky," I said. "What about this House Lilith you keep mentioning? Shouldn't they be putting a lid on this illicit business?"

Mandy shrugged. "Scarlett's good. As long as she doesn't let the humans catch up with her, I doubt House Lilith will care enough to shut her down. They seem content to let the vamp community do whatever they want, as long as they do it in the shadows. At least, that's what Scarlett's clients seem to think."

"But you said they'd assassinate me if I went to a human hospital." I raised an eyebrow at her. "I think their priorities might be a bit skewed."

"You think?" She laughed humorlessly. "House Lilith's job is to keep the supernatural community secret. They're like a cleaning crew. A vamp or wolf makes a mess of things—they're the ones who fix it. People end up mysteriously dead. Strange pictures or events are revealed to be hoaxes. Buildings get burned down. They might even think what Scarlett's doing is making their job easier."

"How do you know all of this?" Laura asked. She leaned back against the far kitchen counter and folded her arms. "I mean, weren't you basically a captive? Did the clients really talk that much?"

"I escaped six months ago," Mandy said, her eyes unfocusing again. "I heard about a rehab center that catered to my kind and hitchhiked there."

"Rehab?" I interrupted.

Mandy grimaced and gave me a resentful frown. "Corralling unwilling werewolf girls is apparently a lot easier to manage when they're hooked on heroin. That's how a lot of them end up dying—if the clients don't finish the job first."

"Oh, God." Laura covered her mouth with one hand and shook her head. "That's horrible."

"Yeah," Mandy said, twisting around in the barstool so she could look at my sister. "That's why we have to stop them. Before they disappear."

Chapter Fourteen

I wasn't ready to forgive Laura yet, but I could tell it wouldn't be long. She'd done the laundry and dishes while Mandy and I had been out. I think what made it especially impressive was that she probably hadn't done housework since she'd left Missouri and taken off for the Hollywood Hills.

David Steckleman had a mansion and a whole staff of professionals to run the place. Though he'd never proposed to my sister, he had moved her in and adequately spoiled her. Just like the last three before Laura. And just like the last three, as soon as her thirtieth birthday was on the horizon, he'd let her go as if their relationship were nothing more than an expiring business contract.

My and Laura's twenty-ninth birthday was coming up in October. Just a few months away. I wondered if vampires celebrated birthdays, and then I decided that I didn't care. I was going to celebrate, damn it. Let House Lilith just try and stop me.

Laura picked up my bloody cup from the table and paused in front of my chair. The worry hadn't left her eyes since Mandy's confession about the brothel activities. The girl had headed to bed early, and now that it was just Laura and me, she looked ready to cry.

"Jenna, what are you doing?" She pulled out the chair

beside me and sat down with a heavy sigh. "I mean really, *what are you doing?* What happens when you actually find this place and these missing girls?"

My shoulders rose up in a tense half-shrug. "I'm a cop. I'll figure it out."

"You're a sidelined cop who just got herself killed," Laura reminded me, gently putting her hand on my leg to let me know her words hadn't been meant as a jab. Just the truth. "Do you have a plan? Are you going to arrest a *vampire* and try to book them?"

I made a pained face. "Mandy says that would be a bad idea. House Lilith rules and all."

Laura nodded. "That's another thing. What happens if they sniff you out? Are you supposed to get...*registered?*" Her eyebrows drew together like it was the most ridiculous thing she'd ever heard of. Registered vampires. I pictured a crusty old ID card with Dracula making an awkward DMV grimace. No one took a good picture at the DMV. Well, except for maybe Laura.

The rattle-grumble I'd come to associate with Vin's vintage Beetle slipped through the walls, announcing his arrival. At this hour of the night, it was hard to miss. I slapped both hands over my face with a labored sigh.

"I called him," Laura said, giving me a strained smile. "I told him everything—well, everything that he didn't already know."

I dragged my hands down my cheeks and stared at her. "Tell me you guys did not discuss my new *condition* over the phone."

"Not exactly…" She chewed one side of her bottom lip. "It was more like, 'She'll be unavailable after sunrise.' And he was like, 'I'd say so.'" She blinked innocently. "No one used the V word."

"Uh-huh." I stood up from the table and headed for the front door, not wanting the doorbell to wake Mandy. She'd looked like she needed the rest.

My stomach churned uneasily from the Bloody Betsy—Laura's clever name for the cow blood concoction she'd mixed me—but I summoned all the humility I could muster before opening the front door as Vin started up the porch steps. He froze and gave me an uncertain look, both eyebrows raised as if requesting my permission to continue.

"I'm sorry," we said at the same time, both following it up with uneasy laughter.

I slipped out onto the porch and closed the door behind me. The crickets were singing, and dew had already begun to settle on the grass. It glistened anytime the fireflies lit up. Summer nights in Missouri were warm, but a gentle breeze cut through the neighborhood, making the air more bearable. I wanted to enjoy it—and I wanted some privacy from my nosy sister and Mandy's super wolf hearing.

I sat down on the edge of the steps and waited for Vin to join me. He moved slowly, his actions more calculated and cautious than before. I tried not to let it bother me. I'd taken more than my fair share of offense with him, and all for something that wasn't his fault.

"So," he said, rubbing his hands over his knees. "Looks like all the cards are finally on the table."

He'd changed out of the flashy clothes and reverted back to khaki shorts and a polo. Though he'd left the glasses at home. I took a long look at his face, trying to see him beyond the stain of betrayal that I now knew to be a lie. His brown eyes were curious and hopeful. They took me in, adoring me in a way that I remembered feeling butterflies over in high school.

Could I feel that way about him again? I watched him, waiting for something to come over me. But all I felt was embarrassed regret.

"I am really sorry about all of this," I said. "I had no idea Laura could be so cruel."

Vin blushed, and his eyes flicked away from mine. "I had no idea she was such a good actress. I feel completely violated. You realize I've spent years wondering what went wrong that night? I went from thinking I was a terrible lover to thinking you had been under the influence of something and had actually forgotten…" He made a horrified face. "If you—if *Laura*—hadn't been so aggressive and initiated everything, I almost would have considered myself a rapist."

"Wow." I hugged myself and shuddered. "I can't even imagine what that must have been like for you."

"Me?" He laughed. "I can't imagine what it must have been like for you when Jason Tanner told the whole school what he'd witnessed at Mooney Park."

I gasped, the final mystery solved. "*That's* why she took you there." Laura had wanted to snoop on her ex—and possibly make him jealous. Too bad Vin had been calling out my name instead of hers.

Vin blushed again, clearly embarrassed that he'd been such a pawn. We both had been. "So, how long have you been a mistress of the night?" he asked, wagging his eyebrows. If he wanted to change the subject, I'd let him. It was a sore spot for me, too.

"Three nights," I answered, invoking a casually humorous tone as I blew on my nails and rubbed them down the shoulder of my tee shirt. "I'm basically a pro now. At least, I haven't eaten anyone's face off yet. So there's that."

"Did you…drink the blood I brought?" he asked timidly. "I noticed you didn't throw it at me like the flowers I brought."

I winced. "Sorry about that. And, yes, I drank it." I

hesitated and gave him a lopsided smile. "You didn't happen to bring any more of that, did you?"

"Sorry." He pressed his lips together, and a mischievous sparkle lit his eyes. "But if you're in need of a donor…"

A tremor rippled through my chest, and I shivered. "I don't know if that's such a good idea. I haven't tried anything besides cow blood and the one bag you brought." I tried to ease away from him without being too obvious. My canines were responding automatically, and my mouth watered.

"I just ate a big meal," Vin said. "And if you have some cookies and OJ on hand, I think we could make this work. Trust me, I'm a doctor." He put a hand over his heart and gave me a goofy smile.

"Why are you so eager to bleed for me?" I asked, trying to laugh off the panic hitching my breath. "It's not like you have anything to atone for. I know that now."

Vin reached for my hand as I scooted to the far edge of the porch steps and angled myself toward him. "I'm not trying to atone," he said. "I like you, Jenna. I have since high school. And if there's any chance that you might feel the same way about me, especially in light of your sister's recent reveal," he added under his breath, "then I want you to feel like you can count on me to help you through this."

"You are helping me through this," I said, resisting the urge to pull my hand out from under his. "The blood bag was very appreciated. Thank you."

He sighed and leaned away from me. "I stole that from the hospital when I went to pick up a body this afternoon. I'm not proud of it."

"Oh." *Crap.* Now I was encouraging him to break the law and risk his medical license and livelihood on my behalf. "Well, there's always the cow blood," I said dismally. I couldn't even fake enjoying that. Ugh.

"What am I? Chopped liver?" Vin asked, mock offense in his tone. He squeezed my hand. "What are you so afraid of? Do you think I'll bite back or something?"

I sucked in a shaky breath as my canines rubbed the inside of my lower lip. An uneasy tightness filled my chest and stomach, and I realized that my body was fighting against me. There was a warm, willing meal sitting within arm's length, and here I was, debating whether or not I should turn it down. That I was starving didn't help.

I licked my lips and stared at Vin, watching the look of hopeful excitement return to his eyes. His hand tightened around mine, and I could feel the sweat on his palm.

"Let's go inside," I whispered, nodding my head at the door.

Vin tripped over the top step in his haste to stand. The red shade of my hunger didn't miss anything. I could see the throb of his pulse, the rush of blood through veins just beneath his skin. Something about the silent invasion made me feel dirty, like Superman abusing his X-ray vision.

I placed a finger over my lips as I closed the front door behind us. The kitchen light was on. It spilled into the living room, providing just enough illumination for us to find our way to the sofa without tripping over the coffee table.

Twin snores drifted down the hallway—through my and Laura's old bedroom door. All of my senses were flying off the charts. I'd noticed the intense smells before. Some were even familiar, like the vanilla and orange scent of my mother's candles. Like Vin's cologne and sweat. But now that I was slowing things down and focusing, I realized there was so much more to it than that.

I could hear the clock in the kitchen and the buzz of the light fixture over the sink. I could hear Vin's breath as it rushed in and out with anticipation. The backs of my arms brushed against the suede upholstery of the sofa, and I felt the warmth of Vin's leg through my jeans as he scooted closer to me. I was drowning in the strange bliss that everything seemed to conjure.

Vin unbuttoned the collar of his polo.

"What are you doing?" I whispered.

He glanced up at me and pursed his lips. "Uh…isn't the neck the best place to, you know—" He gave me a sheepish smile.

I hesitated. "I honestly don't know, but I'm sure your wrist would work just as well."

"Maybe I've just seen one too many vampire movies." He shrugged but left his collar undone. "Is there anything we should have on hand before we do this? Bandages? The OJ and cookies maybe?"

"Right." I stood, suddenly anxious to put some distance between us. "I'll be right back."

I circled the sofa and darted into the kitchen. Laura had put all the groceries away. Other than the Bloody Betsy ingredients, all I could remember that she'd bought was eggs. I dug around in the refrigerator but couldn't locate any OJ. The orange Gatorade would have to do. In the pantry, I found a half-eaten box of chocolate chip cookies. They'd been left open, and while I couldn't taste them to make sure they hadn't staled, my heightened sense of smell confirmed that they were still fresh.

I handed Vin the human refreshments over the back of the sofa and then zipped out of the living room again, stopping in front of the linen closet in the hallway outside my bedroom. My hands were shaking, and I wasn't sure if it was more from hunger or fear.

I didn't know what I was doing. What if this all went horribly wrong? How would I explain this to Laura and Mandy? How would I explain it to the police?

I put my fingers to the side of my neck, feeling for my pulse. I tried to recall my first aid training course. What artery was that? The carotid or the aorta? What was the one in the wrist? Which one was I most likely to accidentally hit? I grabbed a box of bandages from the linen closet and stood there a minute, wondering if I should call the whole thing off.

"Everything okay?" Vin asked. He stood at the mouth of the hallway. The kitchen light split him down the middle, leaving his other half in the dark of the living room. When I didn't answer, he took a careful step toward me, leaving the window of light and joining me in the shadows.

"I don't think I can do this," I said, my voice breaking. I clutched the box of bandages to my chest as Vin shushed me and wrapped his arms around my back, encasing me in a hug.

"Hey, don't sweat it," he whispered in my ear. "I can get more bagged blood—"

"I don't want to compromise your job—"

"I'll find another way." He stroked the back of my neck and then took the bandages from me and placed them on the closet shelf. "Even if I have to draw it from myself. It'll be okay. We'll figure this out." His chest felt warm and solid against me. I breathed in the scent of him and slid my hands under his arms, linking them behind his back with a sigh.

"Vin, you don't owe me anything—"

He stopped me with more shushing and rubbed his hands

in circles over my back. I relaxed, melting against him. This felt nice. Too nice. I was almost embarrassed by how much I enjoyed his touch.

I hadn't really dated since Mom's death. I was sure Dr. Townsend would remind me—or Laura, rather—about that at my appointment. She'd suggest it was another footstep I was following. I couldn't remember Mom ever going on a date while Laura and I were growing up. It didn't seem odd until I really thought about it. I wondered why. Were two ornery girls really that much baggage?

Vin reached up and loosened the elastic of my ponytail, gently pulling it free until my hair fell in a tangled wave down my back. He ran his hands through it and made a soft noise against my ear. Something stirred low in my stomach, and then his mouth was on my neck, laying light kisses in a line down to my shoulder where the collar of my tee shirt began.

My vision melted to red as I took a shuddering breath. "Vin," I gasped his name, the sound a collision of want and fear and warning.

"Jenna," he said, his lips grazing my cheekbone. My chin bumped his shoulder, and my mouth moved like a magnet.

Everything happened too fast. My canines sank into the meat of his neck, and my tongue lapped at the blood that spilled from the two puncture marks. My arms were still locked behind Vin, and I felt him groan as my grasp on him tightened.

I tasted the chemical trace of cologne and the salt of sweat, but it was soon washed away by the bittersweet tang of blood. My lips burned from the heat of it, but I didn't care. It was so good. So dangerously good.

Vin's breath grew ragged in my ear, and I felt a stab of panic. What if I couldn't stop? How much had I consumed already? How much was too much? Then Vin's hand crawled up my ribcage and cupped my breast. He leaned into me, and my back knocked against the hallway wall. His arousal stabbed at my hip, and I was forced to pry my mouth away from his neck.

I gasped as he sagged against me. His eyelids fluttered, and I realized it wasn't just because of the spell of desire. He was about to lose consciousness. He moaned, and one side of his mouth tugged up in a shaky grin.

"Vin?" I whispered, my breath heavy from his weight and my racing heart. "Oh, shit. I took too much."

I ducked my shoulder under his arm and pulled him upright. It was easier than I'd anticipated. With his blood coursing through me, I felt like I could have put him in a fireman's hold and run laps around the neighborhood. *God*, I felt good.

"Hold on, Vin," I said, dragging him back into the living room and onto the sofa.

"I'm okay," he said, reaching for the button on his shorts. I grabbed the Gatorade and cracked it open before holding it up to his mouth.

"Drink," I demanded.

Vin made a disgruntled noise, but he obeyed. He chugged a third of the bottle before I relented and let him take a breath.

"Wow," he said, shaking his head. "Does the room always move this fast?"

"Cookies next," I said, stuffing my hand down into the box. When the kitchen light caught on the blood dripping down his neck and into the collar of his polo, I dropped the box in his lap and jumped up to fetch the bandages.

"Careful," Vin said, adjusting his groin with a grimace. He stuffed a cookie into his mouth and stared at me, his eyes still dreamy and unfocused.

I grabbed the bandages out of the linen closet along with a tube of antibiotic ointment and rushed back to the sofa. Vin didn't seem to notice that half his collar was soaked with blood. But at least it wasn't squirting across the room. That was a good sign.

"Hold still," I said, gooping the ointment over the holes I'd left in his flesh. I unwrapped the biggest bandage I could find and slapped it over his neck, earning a soft groan. "This was a bad idea," I said. "I'm so sorry."

"I'm not," Vin said around a cookie. He reached for my

hand, but I moved out of reach and down to the opposite end of the couch. "If we get all touchy feely again, I could end up killing you."

"Maybe if I tied you up first." He licked a crumb from his bottom lip and made a suggestive noise in the back of his throat. "We can be creative."

"Vin." I felt my cheeks flush at his brazenness and wondered if maybe the blood loss was still affecting him. "You're moving too fast for me. This is all still so new."

"What? I've already seen you naked." He wagged his eyebrows at me, and my jaw unhinged. I couldn't believe he would say something so crude about me in my corpsified daytime condition. *Ugh*. It was just wrong.

"Oh my God." I made a face at him. "Please, don't make me regret this more than I already do."

"Sorry," Vin said. He blinked a few times as if his words were just now catching up with him. "I don't feel so good." He looked down at the box of cookies and frowned before taking another drink of Gatorade.

"I'll call you a cab." I reached for the phone on the table between the sofa and the recliner. "You can retrieve your car tomorrow once you've extracted your foot from your mouth."

"Are you sure you don't want me to stay?" he asked, pouting as he crunched through another cookie. "What if you need a midnight snack?"

"Midnight has come and gone, Vin."

Chapter Fifteen

I did not want to go back to East St. Louis, but when I woke up Monday night and had to listen to Laura's reenactment of my appointment with Dr. Townsend, and her own personal assessment of my mental health, I couldn't bring myself to accept another of her disgusting cow concoctions.

My pride was fragile enough after the incident with Vin. He hadn't picked up his car yet, and I hadn't found the nerve to call and check on him. If he were half as embarrassed as I was, we probably wouldn't be talking again anytime soon.

I could still taste his blood in my mouth. Even after brushing my teeth. It wasn't an unpleasant flavor, but rather a constant, nagging reminder that I couldn't have more. Not now. Maybe not ever. At least not from Vin—which turned into another reason for the return trip across the river.

Let the punks try me this time. They wanted to talk? I'd talk…over dinner.

The aggressive line of reasoning wasn't like me. It brought to mind my first appointment with Dr. Townsend and her initial assessment that I didn't have a chip on my shoulder. That I wasn't the kind of person who would rough up a suspect just to get my jollies. Had becoming a vampire changed me so much? Or was this restless rage coming more from being put on the bench and not having a lead to continue my unsanctioned investigation?

I parked the Bronco in front of the meat shop and adjusted the Glock in my shoulder holster before jumping out and heading across the street. It was just after ten, and the owner was wiping down tables inside, the sign already turned to *Closed* behind the barred front window. I knocked on the door, and his head jerked up.

"Get out of here," he yelled, waving his arm at me as if he were shooing off a stray cat. Then he pointed past the front window, toward the far corner of the store. "That's your fault, girl. I don't need any more trouble."

I took a few steps back, off the sidewalk and past the curb into the street, and looked up at the face of the building. The security lights were angled oddly, and I realized it was to distract the eye from the fresh graffiti dripping down the brickwork.

Wite Bred Sold Her.

I wondered at what age these thugs had dropped out of school. It was hard not to feel at least a little sorry for them…but I tried to push the thought out of my mind. I was hungry. And given a chance, I knew what they'd do to me. Sympathy wouldn't make the meal I was after any easier to stomach.

I stepped back up to the curb and knocked on the door again, pulling out three hundred dollar bills and waving them over my head for the world to see. The shop owner made a pained face, but the money finally lured him in. He unlocked the door and grabbed my arm, yanking me inside.

"It's gonna cost more than that to fix my store," he grumbled as he dragged me past the counter and through a doorway into the back room. "Every time you drop in, the hoodlums is gonna tag it."

I dug my heels in and pulled my arm out of his grasp. We couldn't be seen through the front window now, which had been part of my plan. Of course, my vehicle was probably bait enough.

"I'm sorry about your store," I said, guilt catching up with me. He seemed like a decent enough guy, and I hated being a source of strife for one of the few businesses that were actually making it in this neighborhood.

He glared at me and then opened the door to a walk-in cooler. "How much you need this time?"

I stopped at the threshold of the cooler and gaped. One entire wall was nothing but shelves and shelves of blood. With a stash like that, he had to know what he was getting himself into. And he had to know someone who could help answer all the questions I had.

"How many customers buy blood from you?" I asked, taking one of the clear containers from a shelf. I popped the lid open and gave it a sniff.

The man held his hand up and looked away from me. "Don't…don't do that in front of me." He swallowed and took a half step deeper into the cooler.

"How many?" I repeated, trying to keep the authoritative cop edge out of my voice.

"I don't know. I don't keep track of 'em." His eyes darted back to me, and he scowled. "Some are just passing through. They stop in once, and I never see them again. Others are regulars and come in every week or two."

"You have names for these regulars?"

"No," he snapped. "But even if I did, you think I'd turn them in to a cop?" He folded his arms, and his eyes narrowed. "You can't be comin' back here, girl. It ain't good for you, and it ain't good for me. Don't you have a friend the right color that could pick this up for you?"

My mind paused on Will, and it felt like a sucker punch to the heart. I wouldn't have asked him to do something like this for me. Not in a million years.

I held the hundreds out to the shop owner and downed the container of blood, ignoring the disgusted face he made as he took my money. I grabbed two more of the containers as we left the cooler and headed back toward the front of the store.

"I won't come back again," I said as he bagged my purchase. I'd figure something else out. I didn't need the extra collateral damage on my conscience. I was drowning in enough guilt.

"Mmhmm." He gave me a skeptical frown as he led me to the door. "You be careful out there now."

The streets were empty. I heard voices echoing from several blocks away, and then the sound of glass shattering. Laughter followed. A trace of weed and burnt motor oil lingered in the air. If I waited around long enough, I was sure I'd get what I'd really come for. But the cow blood was already taking the edge off my hunger, even if it was settling heavily in my stomach.

I climbed inside the Bronco with a dejected sigh and dropped the bag of blood on the passenger seat. As I put the key in the ignition, something sharp bit into the side of my neck. A hand clamped down on my opposite shoulder. My vision shot through with red, and I could suddenly smell rancid breath and the week-old body odor of the thug who'd found his way into my backseat.

"Did you miss me, Becky?" He snickered in my ear as his dull pocketknife grated uncomfortably against my skin.

"You have no idea," I whispered, my hunger shifting gears as it mixed with fear and anger.

I snatched his knife hand and dragged his arm forward. Then I turned my head, sinking my teeth into the bony pit of his wrist. He gasped, and his opposite hand squeezed my shoulder tighter, fingers digging into me until I was sure they'd leave a bruise.

The flavor of his skin was distinctly different from Vin's. For one thing, there was no chemical film of cologne. Which was nice. But the layers of stale sweat and the gritty taste that I guessed accumulated when one went days without washing their hands triggered my gag reflex.

Before I'd drunk very much, he released my shoulder and slammed the palm of his hand into the back of my head, rattling my teeth as they ripped free from his skin.

"Crazy bitch!" he screamed. He threw open the back door and fell into the street with a grunt. Blood sprayed from his wrist. He clutched it to his chest, staining his gray tee shirt as he scrambled back to his feet. Jeans that were two sizes too big slipped down his hips as he took off down the alley that ran between the meat shop and the abandoned laundromat next door.

I considered letting him go…but something deep in my gut screamed for more. The compulsion was too much, like a wild creature programmed to give chase if their prey ran. I was out of the Bronco and in the alley a second later, my blood vision locking on to the thug's throbbing heart. I could see it through his back—through his ragged tee shirt and dark, slick flesh that gleamed with the moonlight anytime it touched him through a gap in the buildings.

"Oh, fuck," he whimpered as he glanced over his shoulder and let go of his wrist long enough to hike up his pants.

I moved like a shark through water, gaining speed as I closed in on him. My canines were still extended. The blood coursing through me felt like a drug, and for a moment, I was sure if I pushed off the pavement hard enough, I would fly. The urge to try it was strong. I counted down my steps, deciding I would. *Three, two*—but as I put both feet together for my final push, a boulder swept through the alley and crushed me against a dilapidated building.

My feet left the ground, but not in the victorious way I had envisioned. Uneven bricks dug through my shirt and scraped my spine. I hissed and snarled, feeling all the more like a wild animal, before finally taking a good look at the abomination that had spoiled my hunt.

Special Agent Roman Knight's icy blue eyes bore into mine. His unruly white hair glowed like a halo around his face, dressing him up as the Angel of Death. His left forearm lined my collarbone, pinning me to the alley wall, and his opposite hand wrapped around my left wrist, pinning that to the wall, too. My other hand clawed at his meaty shoulder, shredding the fabric of his black turtleneck.

"Where is your sire, vampling?" he whispered through gritted teeth. "House Lilith will not abide this indiscretion."

The mention of House Lilith added panic to the toxic cocktail of emotions lighting up my insides. It gave me the needed focus to pull my knees up and push my feet off of Agent Knight's chest. The energy I'd built up for my flying lesson hadn't dissipated. It expelled itself into my captor, sending him soaring into the building on the opposite side of the alley.

I landed on my sneakers and tore off without waiting to see how he'd fared against my assault. Maybe he wasn't a vampire, but he was strong. Stronger than he should have been. Mandy would have warned me if he were a werewolf. I wasn't sure what else there was though. I didn't want to know.

The only thing I needed to concern myself with now was getting home and packing my bags. The jig was up—and a lot sooner than I'd expected. Mandy and Laura would not be thrilled, but I'd deal with their outrage over my carelessness later. Once we were safe in a hotel some three hundred miles away from here.

Chapter Sixteen

"You are the lousiest vampire I've ever met." Mandy paced my bedroom as I stuffed a handful of random undergarments into a duffle bag. I paused to extract my strapless bra from the mess of clothes and threw it back into the dresser drawer. Who needed a strapless bra when they were on the run?

"Pack first, bitch later," I said. I'd said the same thing to Laura at least three times already. She was sobbing hysterically from our old bedroom. I didn't know if I could hear her so well because my vampire senses were on high alert, or if she was just that fragile under real pressure. I guess fake murder trials didn't compare to vampire mobs.

"I don't have anything to pack," Mandy barked at me. "Except for my two thousand dollars, which you can put right in here." She held out Maggie's bloodstained vest and pointed at one of the buttoned pockets on the side. "I'm going to shift and get the hell out of here while I still can."

"You're bailing? Just like that? After everything I've done for you?" I zipped up the duffle bag and turned to face her with a scowl.

Mandy pointed a finger in my face. "Don't act like I haven't done just as much for you. This little arrangement has been mutually beneficial, and it was all to help bring down the Scarlett Inn. If you get busted by House Lilith, how is me voluntarily going down with you going to help anyone?"

She was right, but my feelings were still hurt. Who else was I going to rely on for half-baked answers about my strange new existence?

Mandy thrust the dog vest at me again, and I threw my hands up.

"Fine," I said, opening the swinging door under my night table that hid an old safe. Mom had built the piece of furniture herself, and my chest tightened as I considered that I might not ever see it—or anything in the house—ever again. Survival meant essentials only.

I rolled the dial of the safe, entering the combination on the first try despite my shaky hands. Mom had a safety deposit box, too, but she didn't put all her eggs in one basket. That's what she had told me as a teen when I'd walked in on her getting into the safe. I'd been horrified, thinking maybe she was on the take of some illicit deal.

There's only eight grand in here, baby girl. Just another nest egg. That's not even enough to put you through college.

A week later, she'd decided to go over all of her finances with Laura and me in case something happened. Three years later, something did happen.

The safe held about twelve grand now. Most of it was my own savings since Mom's had been split between Laura and me after the funeral. I counted out twenty hundred-dollar bills and tossed them to Mandy. I split the rest and tucked them down into the front pockets of my jeans.

Before I closed up the safe, I removed a small velvet box that held Mom's badge. I packed it in my duffle bag. Then I took one last look at the room and left, giving Mandy some privacy for her shift.

Laura's sobs grew louder as I reached the living room. They were joined by Duncan's high-pitched howl from his carrier. He pawed at the latch and trotted circles inside the plastic cage. Laura's matching designer luggage stood like a tiny, pink city around him.

I put my hands on my hips as Laura dragged another rolling suitcase into the living area. "I said essentials only."

"Don't talk to me in that tone," she said, her voice ragged and nasally. "This is your fault, so I'll pack whatever the hell I want to." She tossed her hair over her shoulder and put her hands on her hips to mirror me.

My jaw clenched so tightly that my teeth creaked. I snatched up one of her bags and threw open the front door. The end of Agent Knight's rifle greeted me. His eyes focused on me through the notches of the rifle sights. I took a careful step back, and he followed me inside.

"No sudden movements," he said. "Drop the bags and put your hands on your head."

Laura squealed, and he swung the rifle in her direction.

"Hey! Hey! I'm the one you want," I shouted and held out my hands while Laura continued to scream over me. "Shut up, Laura! Shut. Up." She slapped her hands over her mouth to stifle her hysteria.

"Twins," Agent Knight murmured. "Of course. I wondered how you were getting around during the day." He turned the rifle back toward me. "How long have you been pulling this act off?"

"Two days," I answered truthfully. "But I've been a vampire for four."

His gun dropped an inch, and he blinked at me. "You were changed when Detective Banks was murdered?" I nodded. "Who is your sire? *Where* is your sire?" he asked, glancing around nervously. I prayed Mandy would stay in my bedroom. I was betting that was all it would take to set this massacre into motion.

"I don't know," I lied.

"You don't know what? *Who* or *where* your sire is?" he demanded, lifting the rifle again.

"Either! Both." I shook my head. "This is all a terrible mistake. I didn't want any of this."

He finally lowered the gun and huffed out an annoyed sigh. "So, you really did wake up in the morgue? That wasn't just a cover story dreamt up by your doctor beau."

"Beau?" I made a face at him. "Vin is not my beau. He's

not my anything, and he didn't have anything to do with this."

"But you feed on him." Agent Knight looked confused.

"What makes you assume that?"

"I saw the bandage on his neck."

I didn't bother asking why he was scoping out Vin. Of course, he'd been by the morgue. He was heading up an FBI investigation. Will was a part of that mystery. Me, too, for that matter.

Agent Knight made a disapproving face. "Whether you like it or not, that means something." He rubbed a hand over his jaw and made another frustrated noise before nudging the front door closed with his booted foot.

"What do you want?" I asked. My heart was ready to explode. Laura looked like hers already had. She cowered in the corner of the room, hands still covering her mouth as tears streamed down her face.

Agent Knight gave us a contemplative glare before sliding the strap of his rifle over one shoulder—the shoulder I'd mangled. Shreds of his black turtleneck dangled free, exposing a chiseled deltoid marred by bloody scratches. I glanced away when he caught me staring and blushed. Blood seemed so intimate now. It felt as if I'd been caught staring at his crotch. My eyes unconsciously migrated there next. Then *he* blushed.

"I have some questions for you. *Real* questions," he said.

I dropped my duffle bag and Laura's pink suitcase. "You

think you have questions? The only other vampire I've encountered is the jerk who offed me—"

"I'm not a vampire," he said, almost apologetically.

"I'm not an idiot," I countered. "But you clearly know a thing or two. I'm guessing a hell of a lot more than I do anyway."

He snorted. "You want to trade information? Is that it?"

"Why not?" I felt sweat spring up on my palms. This was it. I was going to learn something useful—well, something more useful than the scrambled bits of brothel or rehab gossip Mandy had passed on.

Agent Knight squinted at me. "How did you know about the butcher's shop in East St. Louis?"

"A little bird."

He smirked. "A *furry* little bird, maybe?"

"And what if it was? Is there some vampire rule about not consorting with werewolves? I don't know these things."

"So, the morgue doctor, cow blood, and gangsters. That's been your makeshift vampling diet?"

Laura gasped from her corner, breaking her silence. "You've been eating gangsters? Is that how you got caught?"

I flinched at the accusation. We hadn't discussed the finer details of my problematic evening yet, and this wasn't how I'd wanted her to find out. "It was just the one," I said under my breath, a sheepish burn filling my cheeks. "And he started it.

He tried to carjack me."

"Oh, that makes it so much better." Laura threw her hands in the air, sinking into soap opera mode. "You can't just bite at every problem like a rabid dog, Jenna."

"She has a point." Agent Knight glanced across the room at Laura, and I had the urge to move in front of her to block his view.

"So, are we exchanging information or what?" I asked. "Can my sister unpack her things, or do I need to bite at this problem and ship her off to the ends of the earth?"

His focus drew back to me slowly. His eyes were lighter than the navy hue of Laura's and mine. Like glaciers. They were cold and calculating.

"Let's talk," he said.

I nodded at Laura, and she didn't waste any time slipping down the hallway and back into our old bedroom. I waited until I heard the door close before returning my full attention to Agent Knight.

He waved his hand at the sofa, inviting me to sit down before claiming the recliner. He didn't lean back in it, but rather sat on the very edge, his feet firmly planted on the floor, knees at ninety-degree angles. There was a permanent air of distrust about him, and I wondered if he even knew how to relax.

"I'll ask my questions first," he said, assessing the room

as he spoke. He paused on the broken picture frame that I guessed Laura had hung back on the wall and then moved on to the scuffed coffee table between us. He frowned at the teeth marks and missing corner of wood where Maggie had worked her magic as a puppy.

"Okay." I nodded, ignoring his distasteful sneer. "Ask away."

"Is there anything missing from the report that your department turned over to the FBI?"

"I don't know." I held my hands out apologetically. "I was benched after I woke up in the morgue. I haven't seen the report."

He sighed and pressed his lips together. "Do you remember any identifying features about the vampire who sired you?"

That one gave me pause. If Agent Knight were affiliated with House Lilith, then it couldn't hurt to tell him what the asshole had looked like. He might even guess who it was. But I couldn't spell it out for him without exposing Mandy. And I couldn't tell him that there was no need to go on a man—er—vampire hunt since she'd made a three-course meal out of him.

There was a lot to dance around, and I could tell Agent Knight would not be easily deceived. I would have to be extra careful.

"He had light brown hair and fair skin," I said, making steady eye contact. "He was really tall and strong, and—you know what? I can draw you a picture."

"Really?" He raised an eyebrow. Doubting was a fine art for this guy.

"Yeah, really." I reached under the coffee table and found my sketchbook.

The first page I opened to was the half-finished drawing for the captain. A dozen eraser marks stained the image, and the head was strangely misshapen. Any time an online reverse image search pulled up a similar face, I'd changed a feature. I couldn't bring myself to incriminate an innocent man, but the captain was counting on me. So I'd kept drawing until I'd made a Frankenstein monster of a suspect. Now the plan was to reverse engineer him until he looked vaguely human.

"I can tell this is going to be really helpful," Agent Knight said dryly as he leaned forward to examine my work.

I sucked in my bottom lip and gave him a tight smile. "Give me a minute. I'll surprise you." I flipped the page and cleared my throat as I began the new sketch. "So, House Lilith. What exactly is that?" I asked. Again, I couldn't confess what Mandy had shared with me. Besides, I wanted to hear an unfiltered version from a new source.

Agent Knight sniffed and lifted his chin as if he was on to me. His eyes didn't leave my sketchbook as he answered.

"It's the royal vampire household that oversees the America territory. Their headquarters are in Denver, but the duke has a mansion in Ladue."

"Duke?" I snorted. "And you work for him? As a spy within the FBI?"

His eyes flicked up to my face before darting back to the sketchbook. "I'm in a division of the FBI that is privately funded by House Lilith. Blood Vice. We intercept and appropriate supernatural crimes to protect the supernatural community from human interference."

"But...aren't you human? How are you part of the supernatural community?" I held the sketchbook out, angling it off to my right to better recall Raphael from my memory. That was the side from which he'd attacked.

"I'm half-sired." Agent Knight looked irritated by the confession.

"What's that supposed to mean?"

"It means if I die tonight, I'll wake up as a vampire."

I wanted to ask more about how that worked, but his jaw flexed, and I decided it was best not to poke the bear. Not knowing what else was likely to set him off, I went for the point-me-in-the-right-direction approach.

"Is there a support group around here for new vampires? A social hour? Instruction manual maybe?"

"You're not registered," he said. "By law, I'm expected to

arrest you and deliver you to House Lilith."

I swallowed and stopped drawing so I could look up at him. "Why? Have I broken some *vampire* law? What would House Lilith do with me?" The edges of my vision pulsed red as fear bubbled in my chest.

Agent Knight rested his elbows on his knees and laced his fingers together. "You've been hunting in their territory without permission. You'd be sentenced to community service at the very least."

"Community service?" I didn't crack a smile or even blink. I could sense a *but* coming.

"Menial labor for House Lilith—like an indentured servant—is most common for the smaller offenses."

I felt one side of my nose draw up in disgust. "For how long?"

He tilted his head to one side in thoughtful contemplation. "A sireless vampling like you? Ten years, more or less."

"Ten *fucking* years?" I was going to be sick. "For taking a bite out of a carjacker? You can't be serious."

"It's better than being coffin-locked." He shrugged and picked up my abandoned sketchbook with a frown. "Are you done with this?"

I blinked a few times and tried to calm down by breathing through my nose. The drawing was finished and with cleaner lines thanks to my recent practice dummy. I felt pretty proud of my work, even if it was the spitting image of the bastard who had ended my human life.

"Do you recognize him?" I asked, mimicking his detached calm the best I could.

A long stretch of silence followed, and then Agent Knight rubbed his jaw and sighed. "You're absolutely certain this is your sire?"

"Yeah, why?"

"His name is Raphael." He paused to steal a glance at me. I did my best to keep a neutral expression.

"And?"

"And he's the exiled Baron of House Lilith."

I didn't have to fake my surprise. "He's royalty?"

"Was," Agent Knight corrected. His brow creased, and he tossed the sketchbook back onto the coffee table. "If House Lilith finds out that he's created an unsanctioned scion, you'll be looking at more than a few years of maid duty."

"What? Why?" I dug my nails into the couch on either side of my legs. The unfairness of this entire mess was really starting to piss me off. "I didn't exactly get to *choose* my killer. House Lilith, this duke, or who the hell ever is in charge of doling out punishments will understand that, right?"

"I wouldn't hold your breath." He gave me a thoughtful frown. "Raphael and his sister, Scarlett, run the brothel responsible for the missing homeless girls in the city."

"What a family business." I scoffed and tried to bite my tongue before I let anything too revealing slip.

"It's common practice for exiled vampires. They offer an illegal service so their revenue goes unreported and they're harder to track down."

"Well, my department tracked them down easily enough," I said, my pride falling flat. It had cost Will his life, so I was finding it hard to be proud of anything I'd done since making the vice squad.

"I can't believe I'm doing this." Agent Knight's mammoth hands gripped his knees, and he gave me a hard look. "I'm not going to bring you in. I'm going to trust that you didn't know you were breaking a sacred law tonight and give you a pass. Do you think you can manage to find another willing donor or two?"

"Donor?" I blinked at him.

"Like your doctor friend?" He waved his hand in the air impatiently. "You're a new vampire, so you're going to need at least three or four humans in your blood harem. If you know a willing wolf, they're as good as two humans."

"Blood harem?" I blanched.

"Were you bitten by a vampire or a parrot?" he snapped. "Pay attention. I'm trying to help you."

"I am! I am." I gave him a pleading look as my heart flip-flopped hopefully. "I…I don't know if I can round up that many…donors." My solo lifestyle had felt lonely at times before, but never so much as it did at the moment. "Can't I supplement with cow blood?"

Agent Knight made a face. "If you're desperate, for a day or two at most, but you're going to need human blood on a regular basis. Most vamplings share their sire's harem for the first decade or two. You're at a distinct disadvantage."

"Why the sudden change of heart?" I dared to ask, still curious about the repercussions of having a royally exiled sire.

His blue eyes had lost their overbearing glint and just looked sad now. "House Lilith is very particular about new scions, even more so regarding the royal family. The last unsanctioned royal scion that I know of was fed to the sun and delivered to their sire in an urn."

My mouth was suddenly dry. Mandy had been right to fear this vampire society. Maybe I wasn't ready for a social hour, after all.

"What's the catch?" I asked. Call me crazy, but Agent Knight didn't come off as the kind of guy who bestowed random favors for free.

Those spooky eyes of his changed again, sending a shiver through me. "You're going to help me find the Scarlett Inn. You and that pet wolf of yours."

I thought I'd done a decent job of steering the

conversation away from Mandy. Damn. Nothing got past this guy.

Mandy wouldn't like this. Not one little bit. But I was already building a solid argument in my mind. Why not? It was either that or pick out an urn, and ash was so not my color.

Chapter Seventeen

I wasn't sure what to expect when I went to check on Mandy after Agent Knight had left. At the very least, I thought I'd find a busted-out bathroom window. Possibly lipstick hate mail on my mirror. Or maybe even a steaming pile of wolf shit on my bedroom floor. Instead, I found her curled up in the back of my closet, Maggie's dog vest clutched to her chest like a security blanket and a vacant look in her eyes.

"I have to find them," she whispered. Her hair was still curled in loose ringlets that hung down to her collarbone, which meant she hadn't shifted. She'd changed her mind and had hidden among my plundered wardrobe. A few dozen hangers filled the gaps between the garments that had been deemed lame or too mom-ish for her hijacked style, and none of my shoes on the rack below were paired with their mates.

I had to keep reminding myself that Mandy was just a girl. She'd said she was eighteen, but after the case refresher Will's notes had provided, I'd discovered that she wasn't quite there yet. Her birthday was in a few weeks. The Fourth of July. The irony of it was too sad to mention.

"We'll find them," I said, sitting down beside her and pressing my back against the wall.

"But he knows what I am." Mandy tilted her head back and sighed. "I didn't know Raphael was royalty. What if that agent finds out what I did?"

"He won't." I turned to look her in the eyes. "In fact, we're both going to forget that it ever happened. Right now. We'll never talk about it again, and that will solve that problem."

"What aren't we talking about?" Laura asked from the doorway of the closet. She cradled Duncan in her arms, bouncing him like a fussy baby as he whimpered and whined.

"Exactly," I said, giving her a pointed look. "I could really use a Bloody Betsy right about now."

"Oh no." Laura's face pinched, and she cocked a hip out. "I almost got shot because of you tonight. And I'm going to get fingered by a doctor for you tomorrow."

I rolled my eyes. "It's a physical, Laura. Not a pap smear."

"Whatever." Her brow scrunched as if she'd taken offense. Duncan yipped, and she resumed petting him. "It doesn't matter. What I'm trying to say is that I've more than made up for bumping uglies with Vin. So you make your own dinner. I'm not the maid." She left the room with her nose held high in the air.

"What if I stay in wolf form?" Mandy suggested, ignoring Laura's outburst. Her mind was as saturated as mine by the prospect of having to work with Agent Knight. "Then, at least he wouldn't know what I look like in human form. And we could keep looking for the girls." She sounded equally hopeful and terrified.

"I don't see why that wouldn't work," I said. "We don't exactly have any other leads." My breath felt tight in my chest. If I said anything to dissuade her, I would be signing my own death warrant. But if I let her do this without encouraging her to think it through and something happened to her, I couldn't live with myself.

I guessed being dead had already fixed that. Part of me just wished that my conscience had kicked the bucket, too. My heart was getting awfully heavy.

"Let's do this," Mandy finally said, a more determined note in her voice. "If he gets in my way, I'll just eat him."

A repulsed groan escaped me. "What is it with you and eating people?"

She shrugged. "Dinner and revenge. Free buffet. What's so hard to understand about that?"

"Ugh." I glanced down at her twiggy legs and arms. "Where do you put it all?"

Mandy flashed her sharp teeth at me in a cheesy grin. "In my winning personality, of course."

Tuesday night came too soon. As I sat at the kitchen counter, sucking down my third Bloody Betsy and listening to

Laura's update on how she'd FUBAR'd my day, I began to wonder if it was too late to make a run for it. Did Agent Knight have eyes on the house? Would he know if we took off? How far could we make it in the Bronco before we needed to find a hotel with enough protection from the sun?

Most of my concern was for Mandy. The girl was unusually quiet. And she'd only eaten two bowls of cereal since I'd risen. Something was definitely off about that. It distracted my thoughts from everything else, and my eyes kept migrating to her across the dining room, where she sat at the table, scribbling out something in an old notebook I'd loaned her.

"Black or black?" Laura said, stepping into my line of sight. She held a lacy cocktail dress over one shoulder and a low-cut romper over the other. They were both too racy for my liking.

"Neither." I made a face, more at her than the taste of the cow blood, and shook my head. "This is for a funeral. I wouldn't even wear those on a date."

Laura pursed her lips. "You're such a prude."

"Is that a new thing on the west coast now? Picking up guys at funerals? Seems a little desperate to me." I had no delusions about Laura's social life. She might have looked nice on Hollywood's arm, but they weren't married. It would be naive to assume she wasn't sleeping around as much as he was.

"Oh, good grief. It's summer." Laura pouted. "It's going to be hot outside. And my legs are so deliciously tan. I can't believe you're going to make me cover them up."

"*Fu-ner-al*," I said again, enunciating each syllable slowly in hopes the word would sink in. "I appreciate you covering for me and all, but I'm not showing up to my partner's funeral looking like a streetwalker."

"You're not showing up at all." She smirked at me and turned the outfits around to examine them herself. "And he was only your partner for a week."

I blew out a slow breath and gripped the edge of the counter to keep my hands from going around her neck. "He was Mom's partner, too, and he was my *friend*. How can you be so callous?"

Laura's cheeks flared, but she managed to lift her chin as if she had nothing to be sorry for. After her declaration that she was done apologizing for the dirty business with Vin, she'd reverted back to her diva ways. I almost had to wonder if she was glad that Agent Knight had barged in guns blazing the night before.

"He was Mom's partner ten years ago, and I haven't seen him since," she said, folding the skimpy garments over one arm.

"But you're supposed to be *me*," I reminded her again. "*I* would cry at his funeral. *I* would wear something respectful."

She threw her head back and groaned. "I could go in a clown suit, and you'd never even know."

"Oh, I'd know," I said, slurping the last of my Bloody Betsy through a curly straw. "Collins would never let me hear the end of it."

"Speaking of tall, dark, and fashionable, I really enjoyed the run with him and the mister this morning," Laura said, a more pleasant expression taking over her face. "I feigned a twisted ankle and lingered a few yards behind them, and *oh my God*, you could fry eggs on those *ass*-ets."

"There's a special place in hell for your kind." I gave her a wide-eyed glare. "Please, tell me you didn't let them see you ogling."

She made an affronted noise and waved her hand at me. "I'm a television star. Anyone, straight or gay, would be flattered to catch me ogling them."

"Not when they think you're *me*," I said with a tight smile. "You want to fortify your acting chops by playing Detective Jenna Skye? You're going to have to do better than that."

She crinkled her nose, and her eyelids shrank to resentful slits. "I take back what I said about this gig being a cakewalk. It's more like dying a slow, spinster death, made all the more unbearable by the volume of hunks you surround yourself with."

"Collins is gay—and married." I put my face in my hand and silently counted to ten.

"But Mathis isn't," Laura said in a sly voice. My head snapped up so fast I thought I heard my neck crack.

"I swear to *God*, if you put the moves on my boss, I will kill you with my bare hands."

"Fine! Good grief." She turned and stomped out of the kitchen, pausing at the threshold to squint at me over her shoulder. "What about your dreamboat doctor?"

"Laura!" I slugged the countertop with my fist.

"He's here." Mandy interrupted our squabble. She'd been so quiet, I had nearly forgotten she was in the kitchen with us. She stood and sidestepped around Laura. "I'm going to shift."

Laura watched her head down the hallway toward my bedroom, then her eyes pulled back to mine. Her brow creased as she watched me adjust the Glock in my shoulder holster and zip up my hoodie. The Browning was in my waistband, too. Just in case I needed a little extra firepower. I'd considered grabbing the .380 out of the pantry, but I felt odd about leaving Laura completely defenseless, even if she hadn't shot a gun in ten years.

"Please be careful," she said softly.

"I always am." I tried to smile at her, despite our recent disagreements, and she pulled me in for a quick hug.

"I'll wear whatever you want tomorrow. Just please come

home in one piece tonight. And take care of that girl. She's too young to be dealing with all of this."

"I know," I agreed. But it was a little late to back out now. The doorbell rang. I pulled away from Laura and squeezed her shoulders. "Try to get some sleep. I have a big day tomorrow."

She nodded, and her bottom lip trembled as she wiped a tear from the corner of her eye before sulking down the hall toward our old bedroom.

Mandy slipped back into the living room as I reached the front door. She held Maggie's vest in her mouth and dropped it at my feet. I knelt down to strap it around her torso, ignoring Agent Knight's impatient buzzing.

"If I'd been thinking, I would have had Laura buy you a new vest today while she was out soliciting every man in my life," I said under my breath.

Mandy sneezed and licked her muzzle in reply.

I patted her side as I finished adjusting the vest straps and realized that the money I'd given her was still in the buttoned pocket. I frowned. Did she not plan on coming back tonight? Her yellow wolf eyes were melancholy, and I wondered if this was goodbye. We hadn't known each other long, so I tried not to be offended that she hadn't said something before shifting. She was just a girl, and not an overly well-adjusted one at that. Who could blame her for not trusting me?

I gave her a sad smile and a nod before standing and opening the front door.

It was misty outside. A cool drizzle building up to a sprinkle coated everything with a sticky shine. It filled the air with the smell of damp grass and earth. Thunder rumbled in the distance. I hated that I wouldn't be able to enjoy the storm from the comfort of my bed. It was one of my favorite things about summer.

Agent Knight looked like a dandelion under my porch light. His wild, white hair absorbed the yellow glow, comically contrasting with the rest of his foreboding presence. His full-on black attire—turtleneck, tactical pants, and combat boots—was clearly meant to keep him hidden in the shadows, but with a mop like that, why bother?

His eyes narrowed as he realized I was staring at his hair. And here Laura was getting away with eyeballing my colleague's hindquarters for a few miles. I should have asked for pointers instead of ripping on her.

As if in retaliation, Agent Knight lifted an eyebrow at my own hair. I'd sloppily French braided it and knotted the tail into a tight bun at the base of my neck. It wasn't anything special, and though my tresses were a more subtle shade of blond, I was sure the porch light rendered them just as flowery when I stepped outside.

Agent Knight didn't stop there. His dispassionate eyes

took in my thin black hoodie and jeans. As an officer, I'd worn a traditional uniform. Since my first week of vice had been spent staking out a creepy old warehouse, there'd been no need to dress up. I owned a couple of semi-caj pantsuits for the office, but nothing that screamed secret agent the way Mr. Sunny Side Up's outfit did.

"Something wrong?" I asked.

He snorted at my sneakers and then glanced behind me to where Mandy cowered in my shadow. It wasn't like her to play shy. She nudged past me and headed into the yard, waiting just beyond the porch light's reach.

I pulled the door closed behind me and cleared my throat. "Where to, Agent Knight?"

"Call me Roman." The corners of his eyes pinched as if he hated the idea of being so familiar with me. "Scarlett employs wolves. They overhear everything, so we don't want to tip them off."

"Roman," I said, trying the name out. It felt strange in my mouth. "Then I guess you can call me Jenna."

He pressed his lips together and nodded once, just enough acknowledgement to pass for receipt, but not so much that I'd mistake him for polite. We couldn't have that. I gave him a bored scowl and pulled up the hood of my shirt, tucking my hair out of sight.

Roman retrieved a black stocking cap from his back

pocket and pulled it down over his head. It did a fair job of hiding his bright mane, but now he looked like he was ready to rob a bank. I kept my opinion to myself and followed him down the driveway to a black SUV parked at the curb.

"Shotgun," I said.

Agent Knight—Roman—froze and glanced across the yard. "Where?"

I stopped too and blinked at him. "It's an expression. For the front passenger seat. You know, calling shotgun?"

"Right." His brow furrowed over his annoyed eyes and he stalked around to the driver's side. When he opened the back door and glanced across the yard to seek out Mandy, she didn't budge.

I opened the back door on my side and nodded my head at the vehicle. Roman didn't seem to care one way or the other—at least, there was no change in his stony expression. He closed the back door on his side and climbed into the driver's seat, while Mandy crept through the grass toward me. She paused and glanced up, as if to say thanks, and then jumped inside. Her wet paws dotted the leather bench seat before she lay down with a wolfy sigh.

I closed the door and then hopped in next to Roman. "So, this new lead we're chasing, where's the trail begin?"

He pushed a button to start the SUV's engine and pulled away from the curb while I did a double take at the dash. It was outfitted with a state of the art radio and surveillance system. I wasn't even sure what half of the buttons and screens were for, and I'd driven one of the department's newer cruisers when I'd worked patrol.

"Arnie Moreau, who I'm assuming you know is a werewolf"—he paused to shoot a look over his shoulder at Mandy—"gave up a few of the inn's regulars who have connections in the city. We've been monitoring activities around their businesses, and we found a cluster of abductions near one of them."

"You think the inn has set up shop somewhere else in St. Louis and they're still snatching girls off the street?" Man. Scarlett had to have balls big enough to fit in a dump truck. "Why would they stick around if they know you're on to them?"

Roman lifted an eyebrow. "They have loyal clients. And being royalty tends to make them think they're untouchable."

"But they're not. Right?" I was having a hard time understanding why they were still in business at all. Was Special Agent Roman Knight all for show, or did he actually do anything productive for the fancy pants vamps he worked for?

"No," he said, an uncertain crease cutting across his brow. "They will have to answer to House Lilith like anyone else who breaks the rules."

"And this Arnie creep, who was clearly a customer and breaking the oh-so-sacred rules, what was his punishment? Did he make bail like he thought he would?"

Roman's jaw flexed. "He was pardoned in exchange for his cooperation."

"Super." I rolled my eyes. "But I'd get a decade of toilet scrubbing for nipping a gangster."

He didn't have anything to say to that, but Mandy made an affronted chuff from the backseat.

The business in question was a pawnshop near Fountain Park. There was a liquor store on the corner and rundown apartment complexes across the street. One of the reports Roman had filled me in on mentioned a hooker—or rather a young girl *dressed* like a hooker—being chased down and dogpiled in front of the liquor store.

She and the perpetrators were long gone before police arrived on the scene, and no one could say for certain where they'd disappeared to. Considering four other girls had gone missing in the neighborhood recently, it wasn't much of a stretch to assume that they were being held somewhere nearby.

Roman parked almost a mile away from our target. He

ordered Mandy to take the lead. She pressed her nose to the pavement and whimpered as she sniffed a trail down the street. I was offended on her behalf. He should have mentioned that he would be testing her.

I expected the rain to give her some trouble, but she stopped a building shy of the pawnshop and made eye contact with me, her yellow pupils silently confirming Roman's suspicions.

"You're sure?" he asked, drawing her attention away from me.

She dipped her head in a sharp nod and started for the building.

"Wait," Roman said. "We can't barge in without probable cause. Blood Vice operates by a code of conduct the same as the human police, and a random mutt smelling something familiar isn't enough evidence to build an acceptable case for House Lilith."

Mandy whimpered and scuffed her paw on the sidewalk.

"*Mutt?*" I glared at Roman and folded my arms. "Don't forget that *you* asked us to come along tonight."

"I didn't mean anything by it. It's a recognized term for a werewolf without a pack."

Mandy had used the term before, but I'd thought it was just slang. "And what are vampires without a...a pack? A tribe?"

"A house," he corrected. "You would be considered a recluse or rogue, depending on your standing with the house over the territory you reside in."

I harrumphed and followed him across the street and into the shadowy alley between two apartment complexes. It was a better vantage point to scope out the pawnshop. The windows on the second floor of the building had been bricked over. The owner had probably grown tired of replacing glass. The windows on the buildings in worse repair down the block were in bad shape, half of them either broken or missing altogether. The few active businesses that could afford to take care of their facilities had bricked or boarded up everything but the ground floor.

"This position is not ideal," Roman whispered as a car rolled by. I tucked my hands into my pockets and gave him a tight smile. We were just a boring couple hanging out in an alley. Nothing suspicious going on here.

"These apartments look occupied," I said, watching a middle-aged man hobble by with a sack of groceries. "Where do you suggest we find a better view?"

He glanced up at the building behind me. "The roof. We'll surveil until we have photographic evidence of at least two of the inn's confirmed clientele. Then we'll have just cause to call in the cavalry."

"What about—" I bit my tongue, remembering that he

didn't know Mandy's name. "Star," I said, borrowing the first half of her last name instead.

"Stay in the alley and out of sight." Those blue of his eyes darkened, and he gave her a hard look. "Don't do anything stupid. Wait until we have what we need, and then let Blood Vice take them down."

Mandy licked her muzzle and sat back on her haunches. The motion seemed obedient, but the glint in her golden eyes was rebellious and determined. If she caught sight of a girl, she would bolt. I just knew it.

"Maybe I should stay here with her." I chewed my bottom lip and tapped the toe of one sneaker on the ground.

Roman sighed, reading my mind easily enough. "You're too obvious. You'll spook our suspects."

"Me?" I gawked at him. "A few white stripes, and you could pass for the Hamburglar."

He ignored my jab. "Which is why I'm not staying here either."

Mandy pushed her muzzle into the bend of my knee and snorted. Then she hopped up and trotted around behind a dumpster as if to prove she would stay out of sight and behave. I didn't like it, but I'd been outvoted.

"Fine."

Roman didn't wait for any more concurrence. He turned on his combat boots and marched down the alley toward the back of the apartment buildings. I gave Mandy a pleading look over my shoulder as I followed him.

My nerves tingled anxiously, and it was hard telling how long we'd have to wait. I decided to use the opportunity to find out more fun facts about my new kin.

"How many vampires are in the St. Louis area?" I asked as I caught up with Roman.

He didn't look at me, but I could see his bored expression plain as day. "I don't work for the census department."

"If you had to take a guess."

"Two thousand."

"Good God." I tripped over my own feet, and Roman's hand shot out to grab my wrist. He waited for me to regain my footing before letting go of me with a frown. "What do they do with all the bodies? Or is that part of your job description, too?"

"And you're a cop." He shook his head in disbelief. "How many exsanguinated bodies have you come across in your *short* career?"

"I was on patrol for seven years before making detective, Roman," I snapped, not caring for his snide tone.

"Answer the question."

"None. What's your point?"

"My point, *Jenna*, is that I'm good at my job. So is everyone in Blood Vice. We keep the supernatural community from being outed to the general human public, and that can't be accomplished if we allow vampires to go on killing sprees."

"The one that got me must have missed the memo."

He made an affirmative noise in the back of his throat. It was probably as close to agreement as I would get. "Most of them stay in line, but when they don't, it's up to us to put them down."

That was comforting. "And how many of these big, bad vamps have you *put down?*"

He stopped in the middle of the alley and turned to face me, stepping right into my personal space with an indignant scowl. "Why do you care?"

"Jesus. I don't." I leaned away from him. "I'm just making small talk."

"Small talk?" He scoffed. "Half the things you're asking I wouldn't tell my own mother."

"Does your mother know what you are?" The question hadn't sounded so insensitive in my head. Or so personal.

"My mother's dead." Roman's eyes didn't leave mine. "She died fifty-three years ago."

"How is that even…" My brain struggled to make sense of what he was saying. "Because you're half-sired? That's why you look as good as you do? How old are you anyway?"

A shadow of a smile touched his mouth. "I think that's enough questions for one night. We have work to do." He nodded behind me, and I turned to find a rusty stairwell leading up the side of the apartment building. "After you," Roman said.

The stairs were definitely not to code. Some of the steps were rusted so thoroughly that I felt them flex under my weight as we began our ascent. Layers of black paint flaked off the railing, revealing rust-eaten bars beneath. I didn't dare touch anything. I opened my mouth before I could think better of it.

"Can vampires get tetanus?"

"Do I look like an undead encyclopedia?"

"Do those exist? Where can I get my hands on one?" My foot slipped on a dewy step, and I almost went down, but Roman's hands clamped around my waist.

"You can't get tetanus. Use the fucking railing," he hissed in my ear.

Well. Now I *definitely* couldn't use the handhold. Luckily, we'd reached the end of the crusty stairwell.

"It doesn't go to the top," I said, frowning at the crumbling brickwork that spanned at least four feet over my head.

"Stand on the railing. You should be able to reach the roof from there." He crossed one arm over his chest in a warm-up stretch.

"Uh… That sounds like an ER visit to me."

"I'm sure I don't have to tell you that human hospitals are off limits." He stretched his arms behind his back next and followed it up by popping his neck. "Let's go."

"Wait a minute." I held my hands up as he ushered me toward the corner where the railing ended. The bolts were rusty and loose, and the frame sagged a few inches from the building itself. The stairwell platform wasn't even level anymore. "I can't do this," I said, my palms inches from his chest.

If he took another step closer, I'd fall over the railing and likely to my death. *Would a fall from this height kill a vampire?* I couldn't bring myself to ask. He'd already proven himself useless in that regard.

"Of course, you can do this." Roman gave me an expectant look and refused to move out of my way.

I swallowed and turned around, pulling one shaky leg up to rest my sneaker on the railing. It groaned under my weight as I pressed my hands against the brick wall and climbed up.

The alley below was dark. It looked more and more like a bottomless pit the longer I stared. I remembered some rule about not looking down. *Too late for that.* The railing groaned, and then Roman was beside me, perfectly balanced like a cat without anything to hold on to.

"If you jump, you'll be able to reach the lip of the roof," he said.

"What?" I gasped and pressed my face against the brick wall. My legs were trembling so hard that I could hear something rattle in the stairwell below us.

"You're a vampire, Jenna," he said through gritted teeth. His patience was reaching a breaking point. I could tell from the strained ire in his voice. "Jump, or I will throw you off this building myself."

"You should be a motivational speaker, you know that? I think you missed your calling."

"Jump, damn it!"

I swallowed and bent my knees, willing them to steady long enough to do me some good. Then I pushed off the railing with all the force I could muster. As my chest connected with the side of the building, the air whooshed out of my lungs. My palms burned where the edge of the roof bit into my skin, but even as my fingers strained and my shoulders cramped, relief sent a ripple of laughter through me. It came out as a wheeze, seeing as how I didn't have much air to work with. But I didn't care. I'd made it. Sort of.

"Now pull yourself the rest of the way up."

"Give me a minute." I gasped, trying to catch my breath.

Roman sighed impatiently. I felt his hot breath graze my lower back.

"Hey, I'm brand new at this vampire thing. Remember? You don't have to be such an asshole about it."

He grabbed the back of my knee with one hand and shoved me the rest of the way over the lip of the roof. I landed on my face and chest with an undignified *oomph*. Weren't vampires supposed to be graceful creatures? Was that a myth, too? How much was I missing out on by not having a sire to lead the way?

Roman's shoulders flexed beneath the spandex material of his shirt as he pulled himself up using the edge of the building. He was as silent and limber as a gymnast. He drew a knee up to his chest and slid his boot onto the roof, using his muscled thigh to finish the job. Not a drop of sweat touched his brow. I guessed he could do this all night if he had to. I, on the other hand, was still heaving miserably from my attempt that had needed intervention.

"Is that a half-sired super power or something?" I asked, eyeing him up and down.

"Excuse me?"

"The ability to make impossible shit look so easy. Where do I sign up for that class?"

Roman's mouth curled up in a subtle smirk. It was the most amused I'd seen him. And then his blank expression was back in place. What was it about this House Lilith that sucked all the joy out of their minions?

"Try not to breathe so loudly," he said as he stepped over me on his way to the front of the building. "These wolves can hear everything. We can't risk scaring them off."

"You want me to breathe quietly?" I huffed and sat upright, dusting myself off. "I guess that means no more vampire trivia questions."

Roman didn't say anything, which was answer enough.

I stood and patted myself down, making sure I hadn't sustained any overlooked injuries. Then I joined him at the other end of the roof, prepared for a fun-filled evening of gargoyle impersonations and shallow breathing.

Chapter Eighteen

Around one in the morning, long after agonizing leg cramps and half a dozen dirty looks from Roman for simply *breathing*, we finally saw some action on the street below. At first, I thought it was just the liquor store, drawing in the cheap drunks who wanted to beat the last-call crowd. When one of them wandered across the street and around to the side entrance of the pawnshop, Roman pulled out his cell phone.

I opened my mouth to ask if he was able to get a good look with just the dim streetlights, but he silenced me with a lethal glare. I blushed, remembering werewolves had super hearing. Roman touched a few things on his phone, and I watched over his shoulder as the less than stealthy customer popped up on his screen.

The guy was portly and unkempt. From this angle, I had a perfect view of his thinning hair, fashioned into a greasy comb-over that wasn't fooling anyone. His leather jacket looked familiar. I tried to recall the etched logo I'd seen on the back of Arnie's jacket at the warehouse. Roman was likely to know if there was any connection, but from the sharp set of his jaw, I was too afraid he'd skin me alive if I asked.

The screen of his phone zoomed in, and he snapped a few more pictures. I could see the faint outline of a man's face reflected in the glass of the outer door that opened into the alley. Roman's camera was amazing. I guessed it was another fancy perk of his job, like the SUV's exclusive police package.

A gray van was parked at the end of the alley that ran behind the pawnshop, and another man hobbled out of the driver's seat and joined the two at the door. His ratty denim vest held the same logo as the leather jacket. *Mustache.*

It was him, all right, though his arm showed no trace of the bullet I'd tagged him with. The skin was perfectly smooth, save for a tangle of grizzly body hair.

The man just inside the door stepped into the ally to take Mustache's hand in some brotherly half-shake, half-hug gesture. When he turned around, I almost expected to find Arnie. But that wouldn't make sense for the werewolf to incriminate a business he was affiliated with. It was more likely that he had repeated the information he'd shared with House Lilith to his fellow wolf, and Mustache had dropped the hot tip.

The man from the pawnshop ducked back inside and reappeared with a scrawny girl. Smeared makeup stained her face as if she'd mostly cried it off, and bloody knees pressed through torn fishnets. Pawnshop gripped her elbow, dragging her about like a ragdoll, and shoved her at Mustache. She tried to dodge the other man's open arms, but he stuck his leg out.

Her heels clattered on the pavement as she tripped and fell. It looked as if it took all her effort just to sit upright. Even a rookie cop could have easily tied her symptoms to heroin. Her eyes swam in their sockets, heavy lids falling over them as she struggled to stand.

Mustache, Pawnshop, and Comb-Over laughed as she stumbled and fell again. And then Pawnshop dragged another girl out of the building. She didn't look any better than the first had, with a tangled nest of blond hair and bruises covering half her jaw.

"This is the last of them," Pawnshop said, loud enough that his voice echoed down the alley.

"Are you getting all this?" I whispered breathlessly in Roman's ear. If he didn't call for backup soon, I was going to piss myself. My vision was already turning red. I couldn't even imagine what was going through Mandy's mind right now.

As soon as the thought struck me, I saw her. Flying down the alley like a loose cannon.

"Damn it," Roman hissed.

The three men seemed to hear him before they saw Mandy. Their heads jerked up, but she was already airborne. She landed on Mustache's chest, pushing his back to the ground. The noise she made was unlike anything I'd heard before. Even from the safety of the roof, I flinched at the sound. Her jaws snapped in Mustache's face as he tried to push her away.

"We have to do something." I stood and glanced over the

edge of the building. We were three stories up, and the only thing waiting to break my fall was a canvas awning that had seen better days.

Roman grabbed my arm and pulled me away from the ledge. His phone was pressed to his ear, but he tucked it against his chest and bared his teeth at me. "We're waiting for backup."

Below in the alley, Mandy yipped. The sound cut off abruptly, and my breath hitched as I turned to see what I'd missed.

The dark-furred wolf was gone, and Mandy's naked human body lay motionless in the middle of the alley. Maggie's green vest was still strapped around her waist, the fletching of a tranquilizer dart sticking out of the fabric.

I let Roman drag me down behind the cover of the roof's ledge while my blood vision pulsed helplessly. I couldn't think. I couldn't breathe. I thought I would have a better idea of what to do in this situation than when Will and I'd searched the warehouse. I was a vampire now. And I knew what those monsters in the alley were, too. Didn't that mean I was prepared? Why was I still hesitating?

Roman slapped my cheek—softly—trying to get my attention. "Backup is on the way," he whispered. He tucked his phone into the pocket of his pants and peeked over the roof's ledge. I heard the van's engine come to life and twisted around to see what was happening.

Comb-Over was ushering one of the girls inside the back of the van. He climbed in after her, rocking the vehicle until the thing squeaked and groaned. I couldn't see Mandy in the alley anymore, but I guessed she'd been stuffed in along with the others. Pawnshop stuck his head out of the front passenger window and slapped his hand on the door.

"Let's go," he growled.

Comb-Over slammed the side door closed, and the van made a clunking noise as Mustache put it into drive. As it began to roll down the alley, I panicked.

"No, no, no," I chanted, standing up taller despite Roman clinging to my arm in an attempt to drag me down and out of sight.

I wrenched free of him, and against everything that made good sense—including my healthy fear of heights—I sat on the ledge, threw my legs over, and dropped off the roof. Roman gasped.

"Jenna!" He bent over the edge and reached after me.

I turned and slapped at the face of the building, grasping for something to help slow my fall. My foot caught on the lip of a windowsill, and my knee bent in the wrong direction at the impact. I arched away from the building for fear my face would be next. And then the canvas awning caught me. Mostly.

The metal skeleton that gave it its bowed shape snapped against my hips, my spine, the back of my skull. They folded under me like a tent frame, the rotted canvas ripping until a wide hole had formed. I clung to the failing structure as my legs slipped through the gaping canvas.

The concrete steps outside the apartment's front door assailed me next. I rolled down them, catching every jagged edge along the way, wrapped in the remnants of the awning.

I lay there a moment, marveling at the fact that I was still alive, and then wrestled my way out of the wreckage. I could hear the van's engine grumbling in the distance. They were stopped at a traffic light. If it hadn't been for the semi lumbering through the intersection, I was sure they'd have run it.

I took off down the sidewalk, lighting up every scratch and bruise I'd earned from my fall. My right hip was on fire, and a sharp pinch in my side told me I'd likely broken a rib. Maybe two. And something had definitely torn in my knee. I ground my teeth and ignored the pain.

Mandy was in trouble, along with two other girls who had been swallowed alive by the Scarlett Inn. *Fuck House Lilith, and fuck Roman.* By the time backup arrived, that van would be long gone. I couldn't let that happen.

The light turned green before I caught up, and the van began to pull away. My lungs swelled painfully as I tried to suck in more air, and my sneakers slapped the pavement with determination. Before the van had crossed the intersection, I reached the corner.

I darted into the street and latched on to the open passenger window. Pawnshop squealed as my fingers dug into the sides of his throat. I stepped up onto the running board and dipped inside the van, hissing at Mustache in the driver's seat.

"The hell?" he shouted, swerving into oncoming traffic. A passing car blasted its horn, and he stomped on the brakes, jarring my hip into the side-view mirror. I grunted and slammed Pawnshop's head back into the headrest of his seat. I hissed again, baring my extended fangs. It felt like a natural response, but my police training was still urging me to follow protocol.

I held on to the man's throat and released the door long enough to stuff my hand under my hoodie. The Glock would have been more intimidating, but the Browning was within easy reach at the awkward angle. I withdrew it from my waistband and pointed it at Mustache's face.

"Keys out of the ignition!" I demanded. For a second, he looked like he might obey. But then he floored the gas pedal.

Pawnshop grabbed my wrist and shoved my hand into the ceiling of the van. He repeated the motion until my wrist went numb and the Browning fell to the floorboard. I balled my fist and socked him in the face. Blood sprayed from his nose.

A gun fired from somewhere outside, and I glanced back to find Roman standing in the middle of the street, pointing a pistol in the van's direction. What the hell was he thinking? There were innocent girls in here. Not to mention me.

The distraction gave Pawnshop enough time to reach the door handle without me noticing. He twisted in his seat, howling as my nails scored his throat, and pulled the lever, kicking the door—with me attached to it—wide open.

My spine bounced off the bumper of a parked truck, and I screamed. The van door began to close, but Pawnshop gave it another sharp kick as Mustache swerved toward the sidewalk. The light pole was my undoing.

The van door crunched, along with half the bones in my body, and we were both severed from the van. To add insult to injury, I landed on my back, the heavy door smashing me like a bug against the sidewalk.

I could hear the bastards howling their victory as the van's engine reverberated in the distance. Tears stung my eyes and face, leaking into the wealth of cuts I'd collected. I sobbed and choked on my own blood as it bubbled up my throat. I didn't think it possible, but this was definitely a worse death than being bitten in a warehouse basement.

Boots against pavement grew louder, and then the van

door disappeared. Roman panted as he loomed over me. I hurt too much to care about his disapproving scowl.

"Damn it, Jenna." He gasped and then picked up my broken body off the sidewalk. My head lolled against his chest, my lips leaving a bloody kiss that spilled down the front of his shirt. "Hold on," he said, taking off at a sprint toward the lot where he'd parked the SUV.

It was less than a mile, but it felt like a marathon. I wasn't even the one running, but it was my bleeding flesh being bounced about. Roman's body temperature grew unbearably hot. It penetrated his clothes and mine, making me wonder if the sun had risen without me noticing. It didn't seem like such a bad idea right now. Anything to stop the pain saturating my body and mind.

I'd failed Mandy. That made two partners in a row. Maybe it was time to face the fact that I wasn't cut out for this. Could I do that, though? Could I discard ten years of trying to live up to my mother's image? If I died in Roman's arms right now, I wouldn't have to make that decision. Maybe it was for the best. I thought of Laura, and my heart broke again.

Roman came to a stop in front of the SUV. His shoulder dug into my ribcage as he hefted me over one arm so he could open the passenger door. My blood gushed down his shirt, sparkling under the streetlight. I felt it weave a path through my fingers where my hand lay motionless against his back. I couldn't move my limbs. They'd given up on me.

Roman cupped the back of my head as he tucked me inside the SUV. He quickly closed the door and rushed around to the driver's side. Once inside with me, he shoved the center console up and out of his way. Without the support, I slumped sideways in the seat. Roman wedged his arm under mine and across my back.

"You have to feed," he said, dragging my head and shoulders into his lap. "You're a sireless vampling. You'll die if you don't."

Sure, *now* he wanted to share the fun facts.

Chapter Nineteen

Roman's wrist pressed down on my teeth, forcing my mouth open. My lips rubbed against my canines first, but I barely registered the pain. What was it compared to the meat falling off my bones? I was turning to ice. My shivering stopped.

Roman rolled his hand back and forth until my canines found purchase and broke the skin. A trickle of hot blood curled around my tongue. I didn't have the strength to urge it toward the back of my throat. He kept rubbing his wrist against my teeth, like a block of cheese against a grater. And then I found a vein.

My mouth filled, and I couldn't swallow fast enough. I gasped and choked on Roman's blood as it rushed down my throat like liquid fire. My hands grasped his arm, and I pulled him closer to me, groaning with pleasure and pain as my body thawed and knit itself back together.

Bones and tendons made sucking noises as they found their severed ends. Skin tightened as it grew over deep cuts. The phantom ache of wounds not quite healed throbbed once, twice, and then dissipated. I felt like one of those fast-forwarded nature videos that revealed a whole year of seasons in a matter of seconds.

My insides ignited. Every part of me that could want for anything cried out for salvation. And once those prayers had been answered, a new wave of yearning assaulted me. I suckled at Roman's wrist, the taste of him conjuring the most blissful and terrifying moments of my life. The day Mom brought Maggie home. Getting lost at the circus with Laura. Kissing Michael Holman on a swing at the park. Will showing up at the house to tell Laura and me that Mom was dead. Being promoted to detective. Dying in Raphael's arms. And now, being reborn in Roman's.

Roman sucked in a shaky breath and looked down at me, his icy eyes glowing in the dark of the SUV. His face was twisted with torment, and I wondered if he was feeling the tsunami of emotions flooding my mind every bit as much as his blood was flooding my body. I wondered if he could feel the building pressure deep in my gut, the squirming desire I had to straddle him and chase away the terror with more bliss.

This was no timid taste test like I'd had with Vin. I wasn't pacifying a nagging hunger in my gut. I was evading true death. This was messy, unfiltered need. This was everything. Tears filled my eyes from the beauty of it, and I moaned against Roman's skin, my back arching over his legs.

My desire peeked, and then I was out of my head, lost in his blood and crystal blue eyes. I didn't come back down until Roman's hand stroked my face, pushing my hair back so he could look down at me with guarded eyes. The bridled want in them reminded me that he was well practiced at this.

"Enough," he whispered.

That single word broke the spell of his blood and destroyed me. My teeth retracted with a sharp snap, and I pushed his arm away before scrambling across the seat and pressing my back against the passenger window. My chest heaved beneath the ragged remains of my blood-soaked hoodie.

"I'm so sorry," I blurted, my hands covering my mouth in shame.

"Don't be." Roman reached past me and popped open the glovebox. A roll of gauze tumbled out, and he caught it without blinking. He wrapped his wrist several times and then tore the gauze with his teeth before neatly tucking the end under itself. He returned the remainder to the glovebox where half a dozen unopened rolls were stacked next to a suture kit.

I wondered how many times he'd done this for the vampires he worked with. The thought tarnished the moment we'd just shared, and then I felt my cheeks burn as I realized just how one-sided the exchange must have been.

I rubbed the back of my hand over my mouth, trying to erase all traces of his blood.

Roman snatched a handheld transceiver off the dashboard. "Bravo Victor 7-12 to dispatch," he said as he pressed the ignition button to start the SUV.

"Go ahead, 7-12," a clear, feminine voice replied through

the speaker.

"I have engaged tracer ST946 on a suspect's vehicle."

"Locking onto the coordinates now. Do you require assistance?"

"The vehicle's passengers are with the Scarlett Inn—at least three victims, and three henchmen," Roman said.

"Sending all available units to assist."

"Roger. Over." He hung up the transceiver and glanced down the street before peeling away from the curb. I grabbed the dash as we rounded a corner and torpedoed down the empty road.

A tracking round. Of course. It made sense now. Roman wouldn't have been so careless as to shoot live rounds at a vehicle packed with kidnapped girls. He'd probably been planning to tag the van with a tracer all along. My violent carnival ride only served to light a fire under our targets' asses. We'd lost the element of surprise. And all for nothing—well, except for a super awkward blood transfusion that made me feel things I knew weren't there.

The sound of the SUV's thundering engine did little to fill the awkward silence. I suddenly felt like *that* girl. The one who timidly asked after sex "Was it good for you, too?" Except I was still reeling from the experience. How much of Roman's blood had I drunk? And how was he so in control when a little sip from Vin had rendered his brain gooey and zapped his decorum?

Roman was a much larger man than the doctor, so maybe that made a difference where blood volume was concerned. He was also a pro at this, I remembered again, feeling all the more embarrassed by my resentful angst.

I stole a nervous glance across the cab of the vehicle. Roman gripped the wheel with both hands, his attention fully focused on the street as the SUV merged onto I-44. He'd lost the stocking cap, and his white hair shot off in all directions as if that were its unapologetic default style.

The skin around his eyes crinkled, and his square jaw flexed as he realized I was staring.

"The van is still moving," he said, nodding at the GPS screen on the dash. "We won't catch up with them until they stop, even with as fast as this tank moves. But backup won't be far behind."

I swallowed and looked out my window, watching the blur of lights as we hurdled past the handful of cars and semis on the highway at this hour. Before long, we crossed over the Meramec River and ran out of city, leaving civilization behind.

The stretch of I-44 that led the way from St. Louis to Eureka was a scenic drive during the day, running alongside conservation land and state parks. I hadn't been out this way since the last time Mom had taken Laura and me to Six Flags, just before freshman year. Just before my twin had blossomed into her diva self. The drive wasn't the same in the dark.

"Dispatch to Bravo Victor 7-12." The speaker on the dash blared inside the SUV, making me jump in my seat.

Roman grabbed the transceiver again and held it up to his mouth. "This is 7-12."

"Your engaged tracer has dropped off the map, but I've pinned the last checked location to your GPS. Twenty-eight backup units will meet you at the scene and await your orders."

"Thank you, dispatch. Over."

Twenty-eight? That seemed like a lot of manpower for three werewolf pimps. I wanted to ask Roman for more details, but I was still having a hard time finding my voice.

I unzipped my hoodie and peeled it off, discarding the shredded material on the floorboard of the back seat. My tee shirt hadn't fared much better, and it was saturated with blood. A piece of skin dangled from the front buckle of my shoulder holster. I picked it off with trembling fingers and dropped it onto the floorboard, not knowing what else to do with it.

The butt of my Glock was scuffed all to hell. My heart pinched as I remembered that I'd dropped my mother's Browning. I tried to be grateful that I'd been left with the more powerful weapon, but nostalgia still threatened to reduce me to tears. At least, I was going to give nostalgia full credit for that and not attribute it to being within arm's reach of Roman and overwhelmed by the desire to touch him.

I tried to force the aching humiliation out of my mind as I turned the Glock over in my hands, wiping the blood away with the end of my tee shirt as I checked it for more damage.

"Model 22?" Roman asked, shooting a quick glance at my pistol. I pressed my lips together and nodded.

He pulled the console down between us and opened it with one hand, never taking his eyes off the road. A dozen boxes of ammunition were stacked inside, secured under an elastic net. He unhooked one corner of the net and handed me a box.

Roman didn't offer any further explanation, and rather than badger him with questions, I read the label. *Silver Wolfsbane .40 caliber hollow points.* I wasn't familiar with the brand, but if we were going up against werewolves and exiled vampires, I'd take all the help I could get.

I ejected the magazine from my gun and ran my thumb over the first round, pushing it out and into my lap. The spring lifted another in its place, and I repeated the motion until I'd filled my lap. Then I lifted the gun again and pulled the slide back, ejecting the chambered round, too.

The new ammo was…pretty. The shiny, nickel-plated casings looked expensive, and a flowery lilac color spiraled from the base up to the indented tip of each bullet, giving them a delicate touch. It was fit for Barbie. I kept my opinion to myself as I loaded my magazine. Once it was filled, I slid it back inside the Glock.

I dug the extra magazine out of my holster and replaced its ammo, as well. The pile of old bullets crowding my lap fit inside the empty Silver Wolfsbane box. Just as I finished tucking everything back inside my holster, Roman exited off the highway and looped around to an outer road.

The speaker on the dash buzzed with static, and the dispatch operator's voice crackled inside the SUV. "Dispatch to 7-12. Do you copy?"

Roman took up the mic on the dash again. "This is 7-12."

"Units 4-32 and 5-26 are six miles out, with more close behind."

"Thank you, dispatch. Over."

The ammunition ritual had calmed my nerves, and I finally felt brave enough to speak up. "What are you expecting to find out here that requires that much backup?"

Roman braked and turned off the outer road onto a gravel one. It was narrow, almost tapered enough to be considered a one-way. Trees formed a low canopy overhead. A few of the branches scraped at the roof of the SUV.

"I've been investigating the Scarlett Inn for over a year," Roman said, bringing the vehicle to a full stop. "I transferred here from Denver two months ago. Scarlett and Raphael have far more resources than we realized. They've slipped through our hands too many times, and we're not taking any more chances."

He clicked a few buttons on the dash, and the headlights shut off. The windshield and the windows on the front two doors flickered, and then the trees and the gravel road reappeared, all in shades of gray. I could see a driveway ahead that the headlights hadn't illuminated before. It was like my blood vision, only without the red.

"Infrared," Roman said, answering my unspoken question. "We'll be able to get closer this way. Normally, I'd park a mile or two out and go in on foot, but I don't think I'm up for it after the blood loss."

Guilt. I could use some more of that. I sighed and turned to look at him. "Thank you, by the way."

"Don't mention it," he said, almost as if he sincerely wished I never would again. *Happily.*

"What's the game plan?" I asked, offering a much-needed subject change.

Roman eased off the brake and let the SUV coast down the gravel road. The engine was barely a whisper now. "I'll do some light recon, and then when backup arrives, they'll raid the place and arrest everyone on-site."

"So, what? You take the back and I'll take the front? Keep anyone from making a run for it before the big guns arrive?"

"The only thing you'll be taking is the front seat." Roman blinked at me as if he couldn't believe I would even suggest getting out of the vehicle.

"Then why load me up with your dollhouse ammo?" I snapped at him, shrugging off the last of my discomfort.

"In case Scarlett's henchmen find us before we find them. In case this all goes to hell in a hurry." His lips curled back in a pained grimace. "I don't have the patience for any more of your ignorant heroics tonight."

Or the blood, I thought grimly. I folded my arms and leaned back in the seat with a sigh. I'd been prepared to call it quits less than an hour ago. A mouthful of Roman and I was ready to take on the world again. Which would probably just get someone else killed. I seemed to be good at that.

Maybe he was right. Maybe I would even listen this time.

Wait, Skye. Will's voice echoed in my mind. *We don't know how many are down there. Get back in the car, and we'll call for backup.*

It was the reasonable thing to do. All the experienced cops were doing it these days. Why couldn't I just listen? What was wrong with me? Why was my conscience stomping my common sense into the ground?

Mandy. I should have told her to run as fast and as far as she could. Instead, I'd let my fear of what House Lilith would do to me cloud my better judgment. Now, I had a personal investment in the situation. It made the thought of sitting on my hands even more excruciating.

Some things were just easier said than done. Some lessons were harder than others. My dead partner haunting my thoughts didn't even seem to be enough. I knew I'd do it all again.

What if they're too late? What if there are girls down there? We have to do something.

Chapter Twenty

"Do half-sireds experience the red-eye treatment like vampires do?" I asked Roman as he parked at the edge of a cluster of trees and turned the SUV's engine off. The dashboard was still lit up, along with all the fancy features I coveted.

Through the windshield's infrared, I could see the outline of a farmhouse not far off. It was red now, rather than gray, since my panic and agitation had activated my blood vision. I tried to distract myself by falling back on quizzing Roman.

"Red-eye treatment?" he asked, surprising me. I'd expected some useless, smartass retort. Instead, he gave me a skeptical frown. "What do you mean?"

I hesitated, wondering if it was some hush-hush vampire secret that wasn't to be shared with the human help. Roman just didn't strike me as a Renfield patsy.

"You know, everything turns red when you're hungry or angry or scared or…horny," I added, clearing my throat.

Roman's hands were suddenly on my face, his thumbs pushing my eyelids up so he could gaze into my eyes. "Are you experiencing this right now?"

"Um…a little," I said, feeling my breath tighten in my throat as I leaned away from him.

"Have you told anyone else about this?" The grave note

in his voice made me shudder. I'd meant for the trivia question to calm me down. Now, I wished I'd just meditated or twiddled my thumbs. This had backfired quickly.

"No, why?" If I hadn't been so freaked out, I might have considered confessing that Mandy and Laura knew. Not now.

"Don't. It will give you away," Roman said.

I shoved his hands away and glared at him. "Give me away for what?"

"For killing your sire."

My jaw dropped open, and I blinked stiffly at him. "I fired at least a dozen rounds into his torso, but he was most definitely still kicking and sucking the life out of me when I died." And that was the truth. *It damned well better set me free*, I thought as Roman eased back into his own seat.

"Whether that's true or not, you'll still have to answer to House Lilith if it gets out." He closed his eyes and rubbed a hand down the length of his face. "It's bad enough that you're his unsanctioned scion. If they even suspect that you had a hand in his demise—if they knew you bore the Eye of Blood..." He gave me a troubled look and sighed. "Keep it to yourself. You can do that, can't you?"

I snorted. "Only if you tell me what it is."

The sympathy drained from Roman's expression. "It's the sacred mark of Lilith, passed on to a scion only after their sire has perished."

"How does that prove *I* did anything wrong?"

The blue of his eyes darkened. "Scions have killed for less."

"Really?" That was surprising. It didn't seem *that* useful. "Why?" I pressed.

"Your questions will have to wait." Roman shook his head and pulled his stocking cap back on. I could tell he was embarrassed that he'd caved and answered me in the first place. "Do. Not. Move. From. This. Spot," he said, pinning me in place with his commanding voice. Then he snatched the transceiver from the dash and climbed out of the SUV. He reached under his seat and retrieved his rifle before quietly closing the door behind him.

I mulled over the new information as I watched Roman disappear into the woods surrounding the farmhouse. If vampires had killed for this blood vision, it had to be good for something else that I hadn't discovered yet.

I squinted through the windshield and hummed, trying to soothe my frayed nerves. My hands kept going to my gun, and then to the door handle. I tried to come up with a good excuse for leaving the SUV. *What if I had to pee?* That one might have worked a week ago.

The realization that I hadn't used a toilet since waking up from the dead was something that I'd already processed a couple of days earlier. I hadn't made it to that particular trivia question with Roman yet. It seemed like a good one to save for when I needed to remind him that he was full of shit, but I wasn't. It still might not knock him down from his high horse, but a girl could try.

My eyes flicked back to the dashboard as the digital clock clicked over to show 2:45 A.M. Less than three hours until sunrise.

The grumble of engines crept up behind the SUV. I glanced over the seat and saw two cars park along the road on the opposite side. The infrared didn't stretch all the way around the vehicle, but my blood vision—my *Eye of Blood*—was working overtime. I could see everything.

Two agents exited each car. The closest one held a transceiver like Roman's. She detached something from the side of the device and slipped it over her ear before snapping the base of the transceiver to her belt, just above her hip. Then she opened the trunk of the car and passed out vests and rifles. The four of them geared up and then slipped through the same woods Roman had, creeping up on the farmhouse.

I wanted to scream. I wanted to beat my hands on the windows until someone told me why everyone else could rush in and save the day, but I had to sit here like an obedient dog. *Gah!*

Thinking of dogs made me wonder where Mandy was right now. Was she awake yet? What had they shot her with?

I hoped someone had given her some clothes. Then I pictured her in fishnets like the poor girl in the alley and decided maybe she was better off with Maggie's vest.

Something ripped, and I glanced down to see that my nails had gone through the leather front seat. My anxiety was manifesting in ways I couldn't control. I licked the remnants of Roman's blood from my teeth and tried to breathe. *Big, deep breaths.*

My eyes closed, and I lifted my chest, rolling my shoulders back in a relaxing stretch. I'd seen Laura do something similar on her yoga mat in the living room. It hadn't done much for her either. She was still a drama queen. Which was exactly what I felt like right now.

A brigade of SUVs and cars paraded down the gravel road. Dozens of agents sporting rifles and body armor filed out and ventured into the woods. Someone signaled a group to go farther down the road, and they slipped into another section of secluded forest.

They were circling the property. This was the raid Roman had mentioned. It was going down now.

I rocked in my seat, feeling my nails slice through another patch of leather. If Roman didn't hurry, it was going to look like I had invited a bobcat in here to keep me company.

As I squinted through the trees and tried to see where everyone came out near the farmhouse, I heard gunfire. First, just one shot. And then, many. Too many to count. The windows of the farmhouse lit up, conflicts evident in every room. I prayed Mandy wasn't in one of them.

A flash of gold caught my eye—a girl darting across the lawn and through a line of trees bordering the property. My blood vision pulsed, and I realized the color had cut through the haze. But why? That had never happened before.

The wind ripped at my hair, and a single drop of rain splashed against my temple. I didn't remember getting out of the SUV. I blinked and glanced behind me to where all the empty vehicles waited. This wasn't where I belonged.

I stepped down into the muddy ditch and climbed up the opposite side into the meadow that stretched out before the farmhouse. The shadow of the trees glowed like fire. Night creatures sang over the moan of the wind, and somewhere in the distance, a wolf howled.

I'm coming, Mandy.

I ducked under a sagging limb and entered the woods. The underbrush was thick and hazardous this time of year. Foliage camouflaged rocks and downed trees. The trek would have been a slow-going and cautious affair if not for the Eye of Blood.

I could see the veins throbbing in every leaf, the grass pressing up through the forest floor. It was something special to witness, something I couldn't avoid admiring as I navigated my way through the woods at full speed, curving around trees and leaping over rocks and branches, dodging bushes and evading steep hills.

By the time I reached the opposite side of the copse of trees, I was under the spell of my immortality again. Like with Roman's blood, nature had restored me. There was more to this new existence than I ever imagined.

An old horse barn was planted in the middle of a field that the woods opened to. It was the only place the golden girl could be hiding. There was nothing else for as far as I could see, and the distinct heat and thrum of warm bodies shined hazily through the outer walls of the structure.

Tall grass reached my waist and tickled my arms as I cut through the field. The clouds parted, and the moon peeked out for a moment, dabbling light over the barn's roof. The wind kicked up suddenly, and something crashed inside.

A girl cried out, her voice cutting off sharply.

My Glock was in my hand before I reached the open double doors. The aisle between the stalls was empty, but through the wooden doors, I could see skinny girls slumped in every corner, their heartbeats lagging miserably inside their brittle ribcages, shoulders and chins drooping forward and swaying in time with their shallow breaths.

I found Mandy first. She was in a stall with the two girls from the pawn-shop alley. From the steady rhythm of her heart, I knew before entering the enclosure that she hadn't woken from her dart nap, but I had to try.

The green vest was gone, and a long tee shirt had been left in its place. Her hair was littered with straw from the barn floor, and when I reached for her, Fishnets growled and pounced on me, nearly missing in her drug-addled condition. A chain attached to a collar around her neck rattled.

"I'm a friend," I said, shrugging her off. I touched Mandy's check and pushed her hair out of her eyes.

"You're a filthy bloodsucker," Fishnets hissed at me.

"That, too." I shook Mandy's shoulder, trying to rouse her, and was rewarded with a small moan. The cut above her eyebrow was scabbed over, and her lip was still bruised on one side. But I didn't find any new damage. The chain and collar around her neck would be problematic. *For all of the girls*, I thought, taking in Mandy's two stall mates.

"What do you want with her?" the girl with the bruised face asked. She sat with her back to the corner, her arms wrapped around her knees, her entire body shivering uncontrollably.

"I want to get her out of here," I said. "I want to get all of you out of here. Blood Vice is raiding the farmhouse right now."

"Doesn't matter," Fishnets said. Her eyes focused on something behind me, and she cowered in her own corner of the stall. "We'll be dead before they get here."

Musical laughter sent a jolt of electricity up my spine. I turned and stumbled over the straw, wedging myself into the one remaining nook of the makeshift cell as the girl in the gold dress joined us. Blood coated her pale chin, staining her doll-like face, and when she smiled at me, the viscous red liquid seeped from between her teeth.

Scarlett wasn't what I had expected. I'd wanted her to look like Cruella De Vil. Something obvious. But I guess if all villains came with scary costumes, then they wouldn't last long.

The petite girl before me looked younger than Mandy. With her soft curls and glossy eyes, they could have been sisters. Though Scarlett possessed a measure of poise that spoke of another era. Her dainty hands were folded over the front of her gold dress, and a matching ribbon adorned her hair. *If only she'd retained the manners of that era, too.*

Abducting young girls, hooking them on heroin, and then turning them into beasts so they could take more abuse was not a very respectable way to make a living. It would've been easy to assume that Raphael was the head of this snake. He'd been three times Scarlett's size and a force that knew no limits. I was proof enough of that. So I'd been unconvinced when Mandy had said the sister was the brains.

Staring into Scarlett's cold eyes made me a believer. I

understood now. Raphael had been nothing more than a skillful instrument. The innocent-looking girl radiated pure evil.

"You're not one of mine," she cooed sweetly. "But I smell *Roman* on you. How is my little pet?"

Something in the way she said it rubbed me wrong, stabbed at some nagging little knot of jealousy coiling in my gut. I lifted my Glock and fired.

The surprise that broke the civil façade of her face was satisfying, though it didn't last long. Her brow creased, and her eyebrows lifted into an angry mass as she launched herself at me, knocking the gun out of my hand. Blood spurted from a wound in her upper arm, and I inwardly groaned as I considered the possibility that my Glock hadn't actually survived the van incident. At least, not completely.

The two conscious girls in the stall with us scrambled to the opposite side, squealing and clutching at each other. Their chains rattled as they strained against their collars.

Scarlett's fingers pinched around my arms, digging into my skin as she threw my back against the straw floor. I tried to sit up, but she was too strong. Much stronger than her brother had been.

"Whose are you, *vampling*?" She spat the word at me as if it were an insult. Her fangs extended, and blood from her last meal dripped onto my cheek. "I will find out for myself!"

She dipped her face into the crook of my neck and sank her teeth into my flesh on the opposite side from where Raphael had. The mirrored gesture sent a thrill of terror through me.

This couldn't be happening. I was a vampire now. Wasn't there some rule against this? I cursed Roman for denying me so much crucial information. Then I cursed myself for not listening. Again. This was some cruel joke the universe was playing on me. Killing me a second time, the exact same way, for the exact same reason.

Scarlett pulled away with a shriek. She fell on her elbows and crawled backward away from me. "My Raphael," she choked out the word and reached up to grasp her throat as if she couldn't breathe.

I was busy catching my own breath. I searched the straw, groping for my gun and wondering what good it would do me if I couldn't get a clean shot off. I was betting if I put it right in her face it would get the job done.

"My Raphael," Scarlett sobbed again. "Why didn't he tell me he'd set his sights on such a lovely scion? I would have made a good auntie." She sat up in the straw and opened her arms to me. "I could still make a good auntie."

"Ugh." My disgust knew no limits, and I soon discovered that neither did Scarlett's ego.

"You will mind your tongue girl," she hissed. "A bastard

scion will not be tolerated by House Lilith."

"I hear they don't tolerate you too well either." My fingers curled around the Glock. I wondered if I could lift it before she pounced on me again. She was so fast.

Behind her, Mandy stirred. Her chains rattled as she rolled over, drawing Scarlett's attention. Her mouth curved up in an evil grin. "You want this one, don't you?" she said, nodding over her shoulder. "I can smell her on you. I suppose she's pretty in her own way."

I lifted the Glock and pointed it at Scarlett's face, trying to math my way through the adjustment needed to hit my mark. She was only a few feet away. But Mandy was right there. I couldn't screw this up. Before I'd finished the thought, Mandy's chain was around Scarlett's neck.

"How's this for pretty?" Mandy growled. The chain was still attached to the collar at her neck, but she'd taken up a section farther down, likely to keep her head from being ripped clean off once Scarlett freed herself.

Any time now, I thought, the barrel of my gun following the little terror's face. Some part of this felt all wrong. She was just a child. Or rather, she *looked* just like a child. The blood coating her face and the hatred saturating her eyes gave her away, though. My stomach churned as I tried to sever the connection between how she appeared and what she really was.

"Mandy! Get out of the way," I yelled, bringing my other hand up to steady my weapon. My neck burned, and my blood eye, or whatever Roman had called it, was going spotty.

Mandy's head jerked up, and she bared her teeth at me. "You get out of the way!"

I stood, and stumbled back against the stall wall, blinking to clear my vision and my mind. Scarlett's fingers dug under the chain at her throat. She gurgled helplessly and reached for me. *Help,* she mouthed. Her eyes locked onto mine, and I was once again confronted with the fact that she looked like an average little girl in her Sunday best. Her legs kicked up the hem of her dress, revealing white tights and black Mary Janes. The anger in her expression slipped away, and tears welled in her eyes. Her mouth trembled and she let out a soft sob.

My gun was suddenly trained on Mandy, my finger tightening on the trigger. I couldn't let her strangle this innocent child. I had to do something. I had to save her.

Mandy seemed to notice the change in me, and she tucked herself closer behind Scarlett. "Snap out of it!" she shouted. "This little bitch is worth ten of Raphael."

Scarlett's act slipped at the mention of her brother. It broke her spell enough that I was able to control my aim again, drawing it back to her face. She stamped her glossy shoes on the barn floor and let out a frustrated shriek as her fangs extended again. Then she ripped the chain away from her throat as if it had been nothing. Or maybe it had been a test to see if I was delusional enough to fall for her wounded doe act.

Mandy gasped and fell forward as Scarlett looped her arm around the chain attached to her collar. The motion dragged Mandy across the floor. She clawed at the straw, trying to prevent Scarlett from reeling her in. But it was as if she were nothing more than a tug-a-long child's toy.

"I'm going to enjoy sucking you dry," Scarlett purred to Mandy and gave me a taunting smile.

The gun shook in my hands. I was still afraid I'd hit Mandy, even at this range, and my window was getting smaller and smaller. I panted, trying to steel my nerves before it was too late. I remembered Will in the warehouse basement, and how I'd hesitated. The shame burned through me, and I finally felt my hands steady. I pulled the trigger.

Scarlett gasped and moved across the stall in a flash of gold, just barely missing my shot as it blasted a hole through the barn wall. Mandy grunted at the sudden slack in her chain and took a rasping breath. The relief was premature. Scarlett's shock was quickly replaced by rage. She growled and took up Mandy's chain again, whipping it sharply before I could get off another shot. Mandy was wrenched into the air, before being hurled across the stall, right into me.

We hit the wooden wall with a sickening crack. All the air

left my lungs, and wood splintered around my head. Mandy made a strangled noise. I looked down to find the collar at her throat had twisted and halfway popped open. The lock was just barely in place, a small corner of metal digging into the side of her throat. Blood trickled down her neck as she tried to pull the collar away from her flesh.

I gasped and slipped my fingers under the metal band, using all my strength to pry it the rest of the way open. The metal groaned and squeaked, and then she was free. Her skin was raw, and she sounded hoarse, but she was breathing.

"Get her," she whispered, her eyes darting in the direction Scarlett had fled.

I stood and stumbled out of the stall, taking aim down the aisle of the barn. I fired once again, but the bullet ricocheted off a stall door to Scarlett's left. Still, she paused and turned to glare at me.

"I don't think Raphael meant to make a scion out of you at all." She tilted her chin in the air and sniffed at me.

"I *know* he didn't," I said, taking a careful step toward her. "That's why I didn't lose any sleep when he dropped dead."

Scarlett's glossy eyes welled, and her mouth fell open. I took the opportunity to fire another round. This one ripped the bow right out of her hair. I was *so* close. Just one more step and I'd have her.

Thick arms wrapped around me, pinning mine to my

sides, and Roman's irate voice rumbled in my ear. "Jenna! You can't!"

I screamed. The Glock fired into the floor between our feet. His mouth was still moving right next to my ear, but I couldn't hear him anymore.

Scarlett grinned from the back entrance of the barn, unshed tears still sparkling in her eyes. It wasn't a pleasant look. It was a promise that we'd meet again. She gripped her arm where I'd nicked her, and blood oozed through her fingers. It dripped onto her shiny, gold dress and dotted the barn floor.

If I could put another round in her, I was sure she'd drop like a sack of potatoes. But that wouldn't be happening as long as Roman was playing knight in shining armor.

"Over here!" someone shouted from outside. "Surround the barn!"

Scarlett winked at me, and then she was gone.

Chapter Twenty-one

Tears burned my eyes, and my vision blurred as I dropped my gun and ripped away from Roman. In that moment, I was sure I'd never hated anyone more. He was a coward. How could he let someone like Scarlett go free? How could he let her *live*? The things she'd done were unacceptable.

Roman returned my glare as if he had every right to. "Go wait in my car," he said through clenched teeth.

"Or what?" I shouted at him. "I don't work for you—and I'm not entirely confident you work at all. Aren't you supposed to stop killer vampires? What was it you said your job was? To 'put them down?'" I made air quotes as I repeated his words back to him.

"That *is* what I do."

"When you let a murderous queen bee slip right through your fingers, I'm sure you can understand my confusion."

"You don't get it," Roman said, the angles of his face razor sharp from his rage. "And this isn't the time or place to explain. Go wait in my car."

"Or what?" I said again, biting the words off even harder than he had. My bloodlust was just begging for a reason. *Push me*, I thought. *I fucking dare you.*

"Who's this?" The dark-haired woman I'd seen with Roman at the abandoned warehouse broke away from the pack of uniformed officers. She crossed her rifle in front of her chest and rested the barrel in her opposite hand as she looked me over, a neutral expression frozen on her face. I couldn't tell if she was jealous or hungry or just plain curious. *Or a vampire.*

The logical answer hit me between the eyes, as I understood why Roman had tried to usher me back to his car. She could tell what I was. Her perfect poker face was clue enough.

Roman gave me a berating glare, as if to say *I told you so.* "Local vamp that reported the tip," he answered flatly. "She works with a wolf who helped us track down the brothel."

"Hmm." The woman cocked her head at me and smiled. It didn't reach her emerald eyes. "Good job."

A bony shoulder nudged mine, and I glanced down to find Mandy. She tugged at the hem of the tee shirt she wore, pulling it down over her crotch with an annoyed frown. The gash in her neck had already begun to crust over.

I reached up to feel my own neck where Scarlett had taken a bite out of me. My skin was tacky with blood, and the marks she'd left ached and burned. I felt dirty and couldn't wait to get home to take a bath in rubbing alcohol.

"Can I borrow your phone?" Mandy asked, eyeing the officers surrounding us.

I made a pained face as I reached into the front pocket of my jeans where I'd kept the backup flip phone. It was in pieces. I hadn't checked it since the van incident.

"Here, use mine," Roman said, handing her his sleek military model. Mandy mumbled her thanks and stepped away from us as she made her call.

My blood vision had died down, and I finally saw the barn in color—the pale woodwork stained with bloody handprints, the yellow straw, the rusted hinges on the stall doors. The officers dressed in black as they rushed in and out, casting sideways glances at the huddled mass of girls accumulating in the aisle of the barn. Casting sideways glances at *me*.

Roman took his phone back as Mandy returned, and then he grabbed my arm. "I'm going to take them home, Vanessa," he said to the dark-haired woman still loitering near us.

"I'm staying." Mandy hugged herself and gave me a tired smile. "The rehab center that helped me out is sending a bus to gather the girls—what's left of them anyway. They've offered to take them in. I want to see them off."

"Good luck." I nodded and gave her an awkward hug. She was tense in my arms, but she returned the gesture the best she could.

"Thanks for everything," she whispered, her voice cracking as Roman directed me toward the exit.

I paused and bent over to retrieve my Glock from the barn floor. Roman gave me a nervous frown as I tucked it back in my holster.

"Don't worry. As much as I'd love to, I'm not going to

use this on you."

"Thank goodness," he said. "I'd be worried for the safety of my people."

My cheeks flared at the jab, but I didn't bother explaining that my firearm was damaged. I didn't say anything else as we cut through the tree line that ran between the field and the property the farmhouse sat on. I stumbled through the dark, not seeing half as well now that my blood vision was gone. Roman caught my arm twice, keeping me upright, and I grumbled at him for his efforts.

We cut across the meadow and the ditch, and then loaded into the SUV without a word. I still hated him. I still wanted to know why he'd stopped me from taking the shot. I wanted to know a lot, but I'd be damned if I was going to ask him anything. I folded my arms and glared out my window as Roman turned the SUV around and headed down the gravel road in the direction we'd come.

We made it all the way back to I-44 before he finally broke the silence.

"Scarlett must be taken alive." He shot a weary glance at me. "We can't just execute a member of royalty. That's not how House Lilith operates."

I didn't respond. It felt like a vice had been placed around my throat. My voice would spill out feebly, trembling and vulnerable. And he didn't deserve the satisfaction.

"If I'd let you kill her, you would have been arrested and

sentenced to death." The admission softened me, but only by a fraction. There was still so much I didn't know, and he'd been so stingy. If I kept my mouth shut, I wondered how much he'd let slip before we made it back to my house.

He looked at me again and sighed. "I'll return your things from evidence to your captain by Friday. The Scarlett Inn has been disassembled, so we can close the case now."

I almost broke this time and thanked him. It would be nice to have my badge back, not to mention my service pistol and a cell phone from this decade. But I bit my tongue, holding out for more. Roman seemed to catch on and turned the table.

"Your sister might be able to get you cleared for duty, but you're going to have a hard time picking up where you left off at your job. What are you going to do?"

I hated to admit it, but I wasn't really sure. I hadn't thought that far ahead. I'd been content just to survive each night that had passed since waking up in the morgue.

"I'll figure it out," I said, not turning to look at Roman. "I always do."

Chapter Twenty-two

Mandy sat at the breakfast bar, her ankles crossed and swinging back and forth under the barstool. She shoveled a heaping spoonful of Lucky Charms into her mouth and snorted at the K9 manual in her opposite hand. The cover was folded behind the book, and a few dozen dog-eared pages fattened the top corner.

"That's not happening," Mandy mumbled to herself, spraying milk on the corner of a page. I didn't really think any of it was happening, but she'd surprised me plenty already.

If she could pass the practice test, I'd agreed to apply for the K9 unit. They worked mostly nights, and it would allow Mandy to have a job without compromising her human identity. Her picture could still be found online and in various public places, labeling her as a missing person. There were too many questions she'd have to answer for the police—not that House Lilith would let her make it that far.

Laura wasn't too tickled about our line of work, but it did mean that she'd have to cover for me less. She wasn't obligated to by any means—which she made perfectly clear every chance she got. In fact, I was pretty sure she'd only continued the ruse for this long because she was hot for my general physician. She enjoyed the therapy sessions with Dr. Townsend, too. What actress didn't love the sound of her own voice?

I'd eased up on her once Will's funeral had passed, after making her tell me every last detail, right down to the stitching on Will's suit and the number of roses on his casket. I'd wanted to be there so badly. Eventually, I'd find the nerve to face Alicia and Serena myself. Maybe I'd have them over for dinner when fall crept in and I could rise earlier in the evening. That would require some careful choreography with Laura, considering I wouldn't be able to eat anything.

Roman had returned my things as promised, including my Browning and Mandy's vest with the money inside. The items were found in the farmhouse, near Mustache's dead body. At least someone had gotten what was coming to them that night.

I hadn't heard any more from Roman, and I was hoping I didn't. Ever since drinking his blood, I felt all off about him. We clearly didn't *like* each other. I despised him for letting Scarlett get away—and for his theory that House Lilith would kill me dead if they knew who my sire was. It made it impossible for me to reach out for support from my new kin. I'd had to make some hard compromises to find out the things I needed to know.

I plugged my cell phone into the new outlet in the kitchen, right under where the drywall had been patched. It needed to be painted, but Laura and I hadn't decided on a color. It was clearly time to update the space. I'd opted not to replace the cordless phone. We still had the one in the living room though. Mandy liked to use it to check in on the girls in rehab.

"Where are my cork-heeled sandals?" I asked, putting a hand on my hip and turning to watch Mandy stuff more cereal into her mouth. She gave me a bored look and shrugged.

"I have a date," I groaned. "Come on. Why is it so hard to put things back where they go?"

Duncan yapped at my feet, and I looked down to find the strap of one heel between his teeth.

"Laura!"

"What?" She stood in the threshold of the kitchen, my other heel in her hand. "I had an appointment with Dr. Foxy today."

"For what?" I took the shoe from her and propped my free hand on the counter for balance as I slipped it on. Then I snagged the other one from Duncan. "I thought I passed the physical already."

Laura placed the back of one hand across her forehead. "I was feeling lightheaded." She sighed. "I thought maybe he should check me out again."

I rolled my eyes. "He'd better not find anything wrong with you that could keep the department from clearing me next week."

"Oh, relax." Laura circled the counter and pulled a bowl down from a cabinet before joining Mandy at the breakfast bar. "I just wanted another excuse to tell him about your hot, actress sister who is recently single," she said.

"Uh-huh."

The doorbell rang, and I left Mandy and Laura to go answer it.

Through the peephole, it looked like Vin had brought me another bouquet of flowers. When I opened the door and got a closer look, I realized they were empty blood bags. He'd twisted them up to resemble roses, tying rubber bands at their bases to make the stems. The sticky residue left in the bags gave them their dark red hue. It was really pretty creative…and sweet…and creepy.

"Tell me there's a full one in there somewhere," I said as I invited him inside. Vin handed me a plastic lunchbox with a grin. I greedily popped it open before remembering my manners. He was waiting for me with his cheek turned out. I planted a wet one on him before snatching up one of the blood bags and biting down on the stopper to puncture a hole wide enough to drink through.

Vin was safe. He didn't know anything about the dark and secretive world of vampires, and I actually really liked that about him. It made him more objective, and also kept him from freaking out about everything. Roman was too cool and tough to *actually* freak out, but his anxious brooding was close enough to drive me crazy.

Vin didn't know that I was an unsanctioned scion of exiled royalty. He didn't know that my sire was dead. And he didn't know that I saw red on occasion. I did feel a little weird about the science experiments he'd bribed me into conducting with him in exchange for blood bags—which he obtained legally now. Sort of.

The university he'd gotten his doctorate from requested that he give a few lectures every semester, and he'd paid a handful of the students to donate blood for some top-secret research he was doing. Which was oddly enough true.

I'd already discovered, through his helpful little experiments, that I wasn't allergic to holy water or garlic. And I could totally go into any house I wanted to, no formal invitation necessary. Which was good to know, in the event that Mandy and I didn't make the cut for the K9 unit. We could always become cat burglars.

As I finished off my blood bag, and Vin and I headed out the door, the landline rang. It surprised me since I'd had my cell back for a couple of weeks now. I almost let it go, but then I changed my mind and stepped back into the house. I waved Vin on and told him to give me a minute.

Laura came out of the kitchen and met me halfway.

"Freeze! You've reached the Skye residence," Mom's

voice called from the machine.

"I meant to change that," I said, reaching for the phone. Laura grabbed my hand.

"You've made enough changes lately," she said, her mouth curling up on one side in a forgiving smile. "Let's not get carried away."

I grinned as Mom finished her spiel, and then my lips sagged as Roman's voice echoed through the speaker.

"It looks like I'll be staying in St. Louis longer than I expected," he said, sounding every bit as dismayed about it as I felt. "And I might need your help."

Laura gave me a troubled frown as I pushed the delete button on the machine. "What are you going to do?" she asked.

I sighed and headed for the front door. I was going to go on my damn date. "I'll figure it out," I called over my shoulder. "I always do."

Read on for a sneak peek of…

BLOOD AND THUNDER

BLOOD VICE BOOK TWO

Sometimes, when working a particularly shitty shift, I fantasized about what my life might have been like if I'd been a vampire a few hundred years ago. If my sire hadn't been a total asshole—or dead. I imagined him showing me a good time, somewhere like London. He'd be independently wealthy, and by some other means than running a brothel. I'd wear a ruffled dress and he a fancy suit with long coattails and a top hat. We'd go dancing, and then relieve a local doctor of his bloodletting collection. The night would conclude with us settling down in a gothic crypt, where he'd gladly answer my every obscure question.

But, unfortunately, I died in the twenty-first century.

There were no ruffled dresses or coattails here. No fancy crypts. My sire was a prick, and now he was *dead* dead. And I had no one to answer the million questions ping-ponging around inside my head along with all these distracting fantasies. Oh. And now that I was one of the undead, I *always* got the shit shifts. Tonight was no different.

I hated running DUI checkpoints. Traffic was backed up down Olive Boulevard, more funneling in off of the 141 ramps. The heat of idling engines paired with the sweltering

August air was wreaking havoc on my hair and skin. The pits of my uniform were damp, and my legs itched under thick brown pants. At least it was dark. Of course, now that I slept like the dead while the sun was up, it was *always* dark.

The night had yielded a handful of sloppy drunks and one unfortunate bachelorette party that had tried to win over the only gay officer on the force by flashing him. Now that I worked with the K9 unit, I was, thankfully, no longer subjected to the worst of the catcalling and bribery tactics. I simply had to walk Mandy, my werewolf partner moonlighting as a police dog, around any vehicle pulled in for additional questioning.

It was an easy gig, but also unbearably mind-numbing. Like most of the rookie tasks we were assigned. Mandy constantly nagged me to push Langford, the new captain I was under, for meatier jobs. She wanted something she could sink her teeth into. Literally. I couldn't afford to tell her how badly I wanted that, too. And I didn't have the heart to tell her that day would never come.

We had to be careful if we wanted to make this last. The circus act we were pulling off was unheard of. Vampires and werewolves living on the fringes of the supernatural society weren't supposed to draw attention. The more eyes, the more risk of exposure. And House Lilith didn't do warnings. Assassinations and executions were more their style—at least, that's what I'd heard from my very limited sources. It made my occupation difficult to manage on so many levels.

If Mandy and I ever did anything worthy of praise, anything that might make the local newspapers or television stations take interest in us, it could also draw the wrong kind of attention from House Lilith. If Mandy ever bit someone, there was the risk that it could be deemed unnecessary roughness. There was the risk the suspect could convince a jury they were innocent and demand that Mandy be put down. And heaven forbid she get injured on the job.

If a vet sedated her, she'd shift back to her human form. Even if they let her remain conscious for an exam, any half-baked vet would figure out soon enough that she wasn't some rare dog breed. Right now, we were fudging her papers with the help of a doctor Mandy knew in Spero Heights, some backwoods town in the Ozarks teeming with all sorts of strange things I didn't even want to know existed.

"Earth to Skye. Come in, Officer Skye." The walkie-talkie clipped onto my uniform crackled as Collins' melodious voice sang through it, and I was ripped out of my 19th century London daydream.

I stopped and gave Mandy's leash a gentle pull—the lightest tug imaginable. Still, she growled under her breath and turned her black, wolfy face up to glare at me. We were still working out her job expectation issues with the K9 unit. At least she didn't show her ass too much around the other officers.

I huffed out an annoyed sigh before tossing my blond ponytail over my shoulder and pressing a button on my walkie. "I'm here, Collins. What do you need?"

"We're pulling one in, but Ricker and Yogi are still working over the last car. Wanna bring Star down to do a quick trunk sniff?" he asked.

"We'll be right there." I lifted an eyebrow at Mandy. "Lead the way, Princess Pea."

Mandy groaned and grumbled as we turned around and headed back up Olive Boulevard. The white letters spelling out *POLICE* on her ballistic vest glowed in the dark. I knew she hated wearing it in this heat, but it helped disguise the fact that she was no German Shepherd. It also made me feel a tiny bit better about dragging a teenager into my dangerous line of work. Mandy was barely eighteen. We'd celebrated her birthday just the month before, with fireworks and a backyard barbeque, and the small handful of people who knew our darkest secrets.

As we slipped between a pair of cars being flagged through the barricades cutting across Olive, disgruntled drivers shouted through open windows. Someone wanted to know how much longer this was going to take. Someone tried to argue how unconstitutional checkpoints were. Someone called me a bitch. I ignored them all.

The cherries on top of Collins' cruiser flickered over the road, marking the entrance to the lane blocked off for the lucky few chosen for further inspection. Four officers manned the flow of traffic, while Collins and his partner Ramirez questioned the drawing winners, occasionally calling in Ricker and Yogi or me and *Star*, Mandy's on-duty name, to be extra thorough.

As Mandy and I approached the second car in line—a yellow station wagon with Kansas plates—the driver's side door opened. A lanky man with dirty blond, shoulder-length hair stepped out of the car. He wore a flannel shirt and ragged jeans. Our eyes met briefly, and then his attention was pulled away as the beam of a flashlight flickered across his face.

Officer Max Collins was every warm-blooded, hetero woman's idea of perfection. His chiseled chest filled out the shirt of his uniform as if it had been made just for him—or to be torn off on a stage adorned with poles and piles of cash—and his bright green eyes managed to maintain an air of sensitivity even when they smoldered.

"Hey!" Collins shouted at the flannelled man as he circled the car. "Sir, I didn't tell you to get out of the vehicle."

A low growl stirred from Mandy, and before the man could say anything, his attention snapped down to my partner. His pupils swelled as he took in Mandy, and then he was off. He tore past the barricades and stumbled over the median and into oncoming traffic. A horn blared, and he threw up his hands over his face without stopping, until he dropped off into the ditch on the other side of the road. Collins was hot on his trail, the beam of his flashlight bobbing against the nest of trees not far off—where the Kurt Cobain doppelganger appeared to be heading.

Mandy barked, snapping me out of my shocked trance. And then we gave chase, too—albeit, more methodically and without blindly rushing into traffic. As we caught up with Collins, I felt a stab of panic in my gut.

What had made this man so terrified of Mandy? Did he know what she was? Or would he have reacted this way to any large dog? What would he do once we took him down? What would Mandy do?

My heart throbbed in my chest, dreading the long list of

overwhelming possibilities, and my vision was suddenly painted in shades of red. All except for the man we were chasing.

Vampire. He was a fucking vampire. And Mandy knew it. I could tell in the way she was dragging me ahead of Collins. We had to reach this guy first, and we needed to do it without human intervention. But what we would do when we caught up to him was the real problem.

The man darted past the halo of a street light and under a buzzing row of power lines. Then he disappeared beyond the trees. I squinted ahead, using the Eye of Blood to suss out the path of least resistance through the woods. Creve Coeur Creek dipped under Olive Boulevard and ran alongside a small clearing before coiling back toward us and succumbing to the trees and brush.

My guess was that our suspect would try to cut through the woods long enough to lose us and then cross the clearing and the creek. Collins seemed to agree. He pointed toward the clearing with his flashlight and spared me a quick glance.

"Chase him back this way. I'll cut him off when he comes out the other side." He rubbed his free hand over his forehead and sprinted away from me before I could reply.

I pressed my lips together and ushered Mandy through the brush and bramble outlining the trees. Then I bent down and reached for the leash hook on her collar. I pulled her face in toward mine, directing her eyes away from her quarry, and gave her a sharp look.

"We have to make sure he escapes," I said under my breath. "Do you understand?"

Mandy yipped and tugged away from me, but I held firm to her collar.

"This is important," I said through clenched teeth. "If he's caught and held by the human police, House Lilith will hold us responsible."

Mandy grumbled, but she nodded in understanding. Satisfied, I unhooked her leash. She sniffed the ground as I gazed through the trees, assessing the best way to cut off the vampire before he reached the clearing where Collins would be waiting.

I projected my concentration ahead, weaving it through the thick summer foliage. Leaves rustled and twigs snapped, and the vampire's breath hitched as he stumbled over a fallen tree trunk.

"There. That way." I pointed just south of his location. Hopefully we could push him north and away from Collins.

Mandy rushed through the woods ahead of me, but I followed close behind, my blood vision easing my navigation. I couldn't see the creek where it bent around the northern tip of this patch of woods, but I knew it was there. From the higher vantage point atop Olive Boulevard, I'd seen enough to know what needed to be done.

Mandy's growl urged me to hurry, and I doubled my pace again when I heard the vampire hiss. I pulled the can of pepper spray from my belt and tagged a couple of trees before slipping through the brush to where Mandy had cornered our target. They stood frozen, glaring at each other in a tight span of tall grass illuminated by the moon shining through a gap in the canopy. The Kurt look-a-like hissed at me next.

"Quiet," I snapped, taking aim at his eyes with the can of pepper spray. "This works just as well on vampires. Trust me."

His snarl evaporated. "You know?"

"I *am*," I countered.

"But you're a cop." His confused eyes shifted to Mandy. "And you're working with a werewolf."

I shook my head. "We don't have time to play twenty questions. You have to get out of here."

"Then why did you stop me?" The snarl was slowly returning.

"Because you're going the wrong direction. There's already an officer waiting for you east of here, and the school and residential area beyond that will guarantee a full-blown search party." I pointed north. "The creek cuts through the woods and then dips under 141. Stay in the water until you get at least that far."

Another dog—Ricker's German Shepherd Yogi, I guessed—bayed not far behind us. The vampire flinched at the sound.

"Go," I whispered, pointing north again. "We'll buy you some time."

As soon as he was out of sight, I made a wide circle, spritzing every third tree with pepper spray. Mandy whimpered and rubbed her nose into the earth before covering her muzzle with both paws. Yogi echoed her sounds of distress as he and Ricker joined us.

"Jesus H. Christ." Ricker coughed and hacked as he waved the end of his flashlight back and forth in front of his face. His uniform wasn't as flattering as Collins', highlighting love handles and the Marlboro baby he'd acquired after he'd ditched his nasty habit. At least his teeth were whiter these days, and he smelled better. After the initial month of mood swings, he was even pleasant to be around again. "What the hell, Skye? You find a den of bears out here or something?" he asked in between gasping for air.

"I tried to spray the suspect, but the nozzle on my can must be broken." I shrugged and blinked to clear the tears burning in my eyes. "But hopefully Collins got the guy once he slipped out the other side." I nodded my head east, away from the direction I'd pointed the vampire.

"Let's get out of here." Ricker ambled through the trees and led Yogi past the toxic clearing.

Mandy trailed after them, giving me a wolfish snort as she stepped around me. I sighed and glanced north, using my fading blood vision to see how far the vampire had made it. He was almost to the creek. He'd be long gone before anyone ventured that far to check.

When I exited the woods, Collins was waiting for me, arms folded across his wide chest. Mandy sat at his feet, an equally cross expression on her furry face. Collins pointed his flashlight in my eyes.

"What happened?" he asked, his voice thick with accusation.

I swallowed and pushed the end of his flashlight down. "My pepper spray malfunctioned."

"Why did you even have it out? That wasn't part of our plan." He pulled the flashlight out from under my hand and pointed it at my face again. I squinted against the harsh light and huffed out an offended sigh.

"*Our* plan?" I said, folding my arms to match his. "*We* didn't make a plan. There was no time for that. Ma—*Star* and I caught up to the suspect. I pulled my pepper spray, but the nozzle wouldn't work, and the guy took off."

"Why didn't Star follow him?" Collins' squinty, judgy eyes migrated to my partner. Mandy's ears flattened back against her head as she stared at me.

"The pepper spray must have been too much distraction. I should probably take off early tonight to clean her up," I said.

Collins' lips scrunched together. "Uh-huh."

"I'm sorry." I threw my hands up. "What more do you want from me?"

He finally lowered the flashlight out of my face, but as I turned to head back toward the road, he snatched the can of pepper spray from my belt.

"Hey!" I reached for the can, but not before he had a chance to depress the nozzle. A stream of bitter fluid shot the ground at my feet. Collins sighed as I grabbed the can away from him.

"I don't get it, Skye," he said, shaking his head as he walked away from me. "I know you've been through a lot, and it can take time getting settled in a new unit, but you've been off your game ever since you came back. You're not even trying anymore. I don't know how long you can keep this up."

I held my breath as I watched him go, the beam of his flashlight dancing across the tall grass as he made his way back to the road. Darkness engulfed me now that my blood vision was gone. It would take longer to retrace my steps to the checkpoint, but that was okay. I was in no hurry.

I hated to admit it, but Collins was right. And I didn't know how long I could keep this up either.

Read BLOOD AND THUNDER today!

Available in print, digital, and audio.

ACKNOWLEDGMENTS

Starting a new series is a little terrifying. Even with a dozen novels under my belt, I found myself having days of doubt while writing Jenna's first book. Days when I would call or email a friend and ask what I was doing with my life. Luckily, I have some pretty awesome friends who assure me that I am not dumb or crazy for continuing to do what I do. Thank you guys. For real. ♥

Extra thanks are due to my husband, for being my sounding board yet again; my kiddo, for slipping into my office to trade kisses for candy (I'll get those minion smooches any way I can); and my epic critique group, the Four Horsemen of the Bookocalypse.

I would also like to thank my little sister, the lovely Justina Roquet, for being my cover model; Rebecca Frank for creating such a fantastic cover design; Chelle Olson, for zapping this book with her editing superpowers; Kenny Neal, for letting me pick his brain with random police questions; and my new Facebook street team—so many exciting things I can't wait to do with you guys!

I always feel there are a few hundred more people I should be thanking on this page, but alas, I must end somewhere. To anyone I missed (or even if you're a new reader), please feel free to add your name right here: ______________ and accept this gratitude from the bottom of my heart. Thank you for taking the time to read my work. It means the world to me, and I hope it means something to you, too. ♥

ABOUT THE AUTHOR

USA Today bestselling author **Angela Roquet** is a delightfully macabre weirdo. She lives in Missouri with her irresistible BFF husband, their sweet, clever son, and a majestic marshmallow of a Great Pyrenees in a house stuffed with books, toys, skulls, owls, and glitter-speckled craft supplies.

Angela is a member of the Science Fiction and Fantasy Writers Association, as well as the Four Horsemen of the Bookocalypse, her epic book critique group, where she's known as Death. When not swearing at the keyboard, she enjoys playing with her family and reading books that raise eyebrows.

You can find Angela online at **www.angelaroquet.com**

If you enjoyed this book, please leave a review or tell a friend. Your enthusiasm and support make these books possible, and it means the world to me!